WEIGHTLESS FANTASIES

Park yourself, weightless, up against the sickroom ceiling. Spread yourself, formless, across the acoustic tiles. Look down in the dark at the pair of girls lying on the pair of vinyl beds. See how the thin girl curves away toward the wall, pulls the brim of her velvet hat down to cover her face. See how the fat girl stares up at the ceiling, her head roiling with silent plans. See the plans get more and more complex, more and more lushly illustrated, until they play like tiny fantasy movies on the screens of her eyes. Squint and look closely—you can see what the fat girl's imagining: the getting to know each other, the slow sharing of spaces, the slow sharing of secrets. Look at how her jaw hardens as she dreams this, fierce and determined: she is going to know the thin girl. The thin girl has been brought here for her. Whatever it takes, she is going to make their friendship happen.

The thin girl wraps her arms around her chest and tightens into herself like a tiny embryo. Watch how the space between them widens and darkens.

And wait—wait for the bell to ring.

OTHER BOOKS YOU MAY ENJOY

Feathers	Jacqueline Woodson
Hope Was Here	Joan Bauer
The Outsiders	S.E. Hinton
The Rules of Survival	Nancy Werlin
Speak	Laurie Halse Anderson
Thwonk	Joan Bauer
The Truth About Forever	Sarah Dessen
Twisted	Laurie Halse Anderson
Wait for Me	An Na

MADELEINE GEORGE

L**OO**KS

speak
An Imprint of Penguin Group (USA) Inc.

SPEAK
Published by the Penguin Group
Penguin Group (USA) Inc., 345 Hudson Street, New York, New York 10014, U.S.A.
Penguin Group (Canada), 90 Eglinton Avenue East, Suite 700, Toronto, Ontario, Canada M4P 2Y3
(a division of Pearson Penguin Canada Inc.)
Penguin Books Ltd, 80 Strand, London WC2R 0RL, England
Penguin Ireland, 25 St Stephen's Green, Dublin 2, Ireland (a division of Penguin Books Ltd)
Penguin Group (Australia), 250 Camberwell Road, Camberwell, Victoria 3124, Australia
(a division of Pearson Australia Group Pty Ltd)
Penguin Books India Pvt Ltd, 11 Community Centre,
Panchsheel Park, New Delhi - 110 017, India
Penguin Group (NZ), 67 Apollo Drive, Rosedale, North Shore 0632, New Zealand
(a division of Pearson New Zealand Ltd)
Penguin Books (South Africa) (Pty) Ltd, 24 Sturdee Avenue,
Rosebank, Johannesburg 2196, South Africa

Registered Offices: Penguin Books Ltd, 80 Strand, London WC2R 0RL, England

First published in the United States of America by Viking,
a member of Penguin Group (USA) Inc., 2008
Published by Speak, an imprint of Penguin Group (USA) Inc., 2009

3 5 7 9 10 8 6 4 2

Copyright © Madeleine George, 2008
All rights reserved

THE LIBRARY OF CONGRESS HAS CATALOGED THE VIKING EDITION AS FOLLOWS:
George, Madeleine.
Looks / by Madeleine George.
p. cm.
Summary: Two high school girls, one an anorexic poet and
the other an obese loner, form an unlikely friendship.
ISBN: 978-0-670-06167-9 (hardcover)
[1. Body image—Fiction. 2. Eating disorders—Fiction. 3. Anorexia—Fiction. 4. Obesity—Fiction.
5. Friendship—Fiction. 6. High schools—Fiction. 7. Schools—Fiction.] I. Title.
PZ7.G293346Lo 2008
[Fic]—dc22   2007038218

SPEAK ISBN 978-0-14-241419-4

Printed in the United States of America

for my family

• 1 •

Start in the sky. Look down at the valley. Green, plush, peaceful landscape. Drop down a little, toward the town, then skim over it, past the low beige buildings of the university, the clean white spires of the Congregational churches, the flat green welcome mat of the town common, out toward the edge of town, toward Valley Regional High School, a rambling, one-story brick building surrounded by soccer fields, field hockey fields, football fields, parking lots. Hover above Valley Regional High. Watch the crowd of kids as it streams into the school like water sucked down a storm drain. And listen: even from this high up you can hear the hum of a school on the first day back in September.

Now drop, plummet straight down like a stone, through the pebbly roof and the air-conditioning ducts and the bundles of wiring and the soft acoustic tiles, until you burst into the teeming front hall of the school. Float up by the ceiling where you can take it all in, the blended smoothie of backpacks and T-shirts and freckled shoulders and tank tops, ponytails and crew cuts and hoop earrings and knotted leather necklaces. Wince at the noise, the crashing surf of screeching, laughing, yelling.

Now pivot, face the light blue cinder-block wall next to the main doors of the school. Someone is standing there, pressed into the auditorium door alcove, someone so huge and still she might be mistaken for a piece of architecture if it weren't for the sky blue windbreaker that marks her as human, the backpack sitting limply on the floor by her feet.

Look at her. Nobody else is, but you look at her. Look at Meghan Ball.

Meghan's head is tipped down, the low fringe of her mousebrown bangs concealing her face, but her eyes are open. From this close you can see they are a silvery gray, as live and shimmery as beads of mercury, and they're darting back and forth like laser scanners. No one may be looking at Meghan Ball, but Meghan Ball is looking at everyone.

Through the veil of her hair, Meghan sees Tamara Scales press her purple-painted fingertips into Ashley Hobart's pale arm, sees Ashley lean in to catch Tamara's whisper (so Ashley must have forgiven Tamara for making out with Curtis Yazbek—or are they just faking being friends?), sees Randy Ryman biff the bill of Tim Court's baseball cap (Randy's still trying to kiss up to Tim after Tim took the fall for that Motel 6 party the cops busted), sees Debbie Fillipi reach out and grab the hand of a new girl with too much eyeliner on, sees Jenn Massey, Debbie Fillipi's best friend, take a step back, fake a hard smile (new girl must be Jenn's replacement, payback for Jenn spreading it around that Debbie got a nose job in seventh grade . . .). Wrist snap, high five, smirk, hug, nod—Meghan records every gesture, every flick of every kid's eye, incorporates it into her information collection, the vast archive of Facts about People she maintains in her mind.

If she could, Meghan would stay here all day, wedged out of the way, safely overlooked, perfectly situated to scan and gather. But the first bell rings, roasts the air, and Meghan knows she only has two more minutes before she will be forced to head to homeroom.

Meghan Ball is at once the most visible and invisible person in school. In the obvious way, she is unbearably visible. She takes up the most space of any person in the entire school—in the entire town, in fact. She is impossible to overlook in class pictures or on the risers during chorus concerts—they always make her stand in the back row, where her round head hovers above a space big enough to accommodate three normal-sized kids. She has a back as wide as a basketball backboard, perfect for spitting on and pelting things at. In this way, Meghan is a walking bull's-eye target.

But then, just when she feels like she can't get any bigger, when she's feeling brontosaurically huge and exposed, someone will walk right past her—*right* past her—saying something totally private they would never want anyone else to hear, just as if Meghan wasn't there at all—like right now, right this very second, watch:

Kaitlyn Carmigan—bleached and bronzed from a summer spent at her family's place in Maine—pulls out of the crowd, dragging sweet-but-dumb Jessie Sturm by the arm. She hustles Jessie over to the sports trophy case, about twelve and a half inches away from where Meghan is standing. Kaitlyn's flushed face is buzzing with a secret—she huddles up with Jessie, her back to Meghan, but speaks in a voice so clear and excited that Meghan has no trouble hearing every word she says.

"You *heard* about Liz." A statement, not a question—that way when Jessie says no, Kaitlyn gets to act all shocked and sorry for her. Meghan floats an inch closer to the trophy case, then another.

"Um . . ." Jessie shrugs pitifully.

"You haven't heard about *Liz*?" Here it comes. "Oh my God, I can't be*lieve* you haven't heard about Liz!"

"What about Liz? What happened to Liz?"

"Okay, *guess* where Liz was all summer long?"

"Um . . . violin camp?"

"That's what she *told* people."

"But I got a postcard from her from New Hampshire. . . ." Jessie looks miserable, wracked with the agony of being the last to know. Meghan slides another silent inch closer—she's no more than half a foot away from them now.

"Yeah, she totally *was* in New Hampshire, but no *way* was she at music camp. Hannah went to see Justin at Camp Allegro, 'cause you know Justin plays like the oboe or whatever, and Liz was absolutely not there and Justin said she hadn't been there all summer."

"So where was she?"

Kaitlyn pauses for maximum drama.

"*Fat* camp."

Meghan feels the bottom of her stomach drop out—a guilty lurch, like she's just been caught breaking a rule. That word is like a swear word meant just for her; it's like another name for her in this school.

"What?" Jessie cries, crestfallen and confused. "But . . . I mean . . . but Liz isn't fat. Not fat enough for fat camp, anyway."

"She didn't *used* to be. But did you see her yet today?"

Jessie shakes her head.

"Well I totally heard that girls at fat camp are experts at sneaking junk food, and I guess it is so true—you *have* to see her. She is *totally* ten pounds fatter than last year."

"I can't believe she didn't tell me," Jessie murmurs.

"Yeah, well, she didn't tell anybody. And you can't tell her you know, okay? It's a total secret. Hannah said we have to pretend we don't know."

Jessie nods, eyes wide. "Okay," she says.

"Okay!" says Kaitlyn brightly, moving away from the trophy case, passing so close to Meghan she almost brushes against her windbreaker. "So who do you have for homeroom this year?"

It's amazing what people will say right in front of you when you're obese, like you're deaf or something, like you're retarded. Or like you don't even speak the language, like you're a tourist lost in the land of the thin.

The second bell rings, a metallic howl.

Reluctantly Meghan breaks away from the wall, like an ice shelf breaking off the Antarctic. She moves like a glacier, silent and slow. She shrinks away from all physical contact, zeroes out her eyes. In this way she makes it along the not-too-crowded east corridor, then down the steps, then through the fire doors into the packed sophomore hall.

She shoulders through the crowd, blacking out her peripheral vision so that all she can see, at the end of the dark tunnel in front of her, is her goal: homeroom, C23. She is getting closer, closer, having no particular feelings, when she senses the light, feathery jostle behind her, hears the quiet laughs sucked up the nose into snorts that let her know they're massing at her back.

They can't be more than eight inches away from her. If she turned around she could look them right in the eye—but she doesn't know what they would do if she turned around, since turning around is not in the script she and they have co-written and somehow, tacitly, agreed to perform. Anyway she doesn't need to turn around, because she knows exactly who it is back there, can imagine in sharp-focus detail their Red Sox caps, their Abercrombie shirts, the spiky bangs jutting out over their grinning, Cape Cod–tanned faces. It's essentially the same pack of ten boys who've been making Meghan their ritual sacrifice object since seventh grade. Some subset of the ten is back there right now: Chris and/or Matt G. and/or Matt T., maybe one or both of the Farmington twins, and/or Jared and/or Shane and/or Mike and/or Freedom. (Freedom Falcon, whose hippie mom must curse the Goddess every day for sending her such an evil, meatheaded son.) And their leader, J-Bar. J-Bar's always there.

She feels J-Bar slide up against her back now, bring his humming blond head down next to her ear. His voice oozes out of him like rancid caramel.

"I want you to have my babies, Butter Ball."

A wave of hissing snorts and chuckles from the guys.

"Don't you want to have my babies? Come on, gorgeous, you know you want me. Say you want me. Tell me you *want* me, Butter Ball."

C23 passes on her left but she can't stop, can't turn, can't even speed up when they're on her like this. Just go, go, steady, steady, until they decide they're done and they peel off and dissolve.

"I bet you feel like a big waterbed, don't you, beautiful. I just want to flop down on top of you and bounce all night long, boing, boing, boing—"

"Jay!" Samantha Suglia, J-Bar's sunny-faced, honey-haired field-hockey girlfriend, calls to him from the door to C29.

"Yo, Sam," J-Bar says in his public voice, deep and resonant, empty of all the rust and sewage that trickles through the voice he uses on Meghan.

Like a school of fish the boys turn toward Samantha. Meghan is forgotten, freed as suddenly as she was snared, and she accelerates to make it the long way around to homeroom—can't risk backtracking, can't risk facing them again—before the third bell rings.

Homeroom is as loud as feeding time at the pound. Every ex-freshman, every fresh sophomore from Zoe Abbott to Steve Czarniewski is penned into C23, sitting on each other's desks, comparing new piercings, telling summer stories, squealing and yelping and chattering and laughing. Mr. Cox stands, huge and bald and mute as a nightclub bouncer, at the front of the room, his massive arms hanging limp from his shoulders.

"Settle down now," he rumbles. Nobody even turns in his direction. "Come on now, I need butts in seats, people."

Facts about Mr. Cox: He's the head of phys. ed., the varsity and JV basketball coach, and, improbably, the teacher of tenth-grade health. He's very into the martial arts (Jackie Chan is his personal idol) and for one quarter a year, when he's teaching self-defense, he makes everybody call him Sensei Cox. Unlike most guys who shave their heads, he didn't do it to disguise the fact that he was losing his hair. He shaved off his whole head of thick salt-and-pepper hair all of a sudden, along with his eyebrows and arm hair and presumably—ack—every other hair on his body, one day last winter after his wife left him for the basketball coach of Gateway Regional High, right after Gateway beat Valley Regional in the semifinals. Since then Mr. Cox's eyes have had a clogged, stupid look, kind of like a pair of tiny glazed doughnuts.

The door swings open and J-Bar strides through it, grinning and glowing like he's running for Congress. In her seat at the back corner of the room, Meghan takes a deep breath and disappears. But it's a reflex, not a real precaution—J-Bar's not remotely interested in her in homeroom and never has been in all the years they've had it together. J-Bar shouts, "Coach!" and crosses to Mr. Cox, puts his arm around his shoulders like he's greeting his favorite uncle. The noise in C23 rises from a gabble to a roar. Then a blast of static from the PA speaker above the blackboard stuns everyone into a mid-sentence silence. Even J-Bar drops obediently into his seat.

"Welcome students. And staff. Of Valley Regional High to day one of a new year," drones the nasal voice of Ms. Champoux, the pit bull in a perm and polyester blazer who commands the meek team of secretaries in the front office.

Ms. Champoux ("like the hair soap," Meghan once heard her say flatly) is fierce in person, but over the PA she has the voice of a depressed Muppet, piped through the nose and totally toneless, never rising or falling even to indicate the beginning or end of a sentence. She reads the morning announcements like a first-grader reading a picture book aloud, pausing in places that don't make sense and pronouncing *a* like *eh* and *the* like *thee*. She is also cataclysmically bad at pronouncing people's names—so bad it's almost like she does it on purpose. Even normal names get mangled in Ms. Champoux's announcements: Michael Andrews becomes Michelle Anderwise, Jenny Harwood becomes Jeannie Whoreweed—and forget about poor Rogelia Jaramillo and Xibai Qing.

Facts about Ms. Champoux: Her secret dream in life is to work in the criminal justice system as a cop or parole officer or maybe a prison guard. She loves the police shows on TV, memorizes all their tough, hard-bitten jargon and actually uses it in daily life—more than once Meghan has heard her refer to the sullen kids splayed out on the orange plastic chairs outside the principal's office as *perps*.

Ms. Champoux hates her job; Ms. Champoux hates reading the morning announcements; Ms. Champoux is terrible at reading the morning announcements. If Valley Regional High were a humane institution, someone would tap Ms. Champoux on her shoulder-padded shoulder and lead her gently away from the PA mike, sit her down to a task she was actually good at, like detecting the forgeries among the day's absence notes. But Valley Regional High is not a humane institution. It's more like a cruel and unusual penal colony in which every inmate and every guard is punished, each according to his deepest fear. Thus Ms. Champoux, world's worst public speaker, is assigned the task—till the day she dies—of reading out the morning announcements.

"I have an exciting. Announcement to make. After meeting over thee summer with representatives from thee English department our principal Dr. Dempsey. Has decided to institute a new meditation period as part of morning announcements. Every morning we will share eh. Short inspirational poem by eh. Well-known writer followed by eh thirty-second silent meditation period during which students and staff are invited to think about what. Thee poem means to them. Dr. Dempsey does ask that students respect thee silent thirty-second period and keep it—" Ms. Champoux falters. "Silent." She breathes for a second, heavily. "To kick off thee first day of this exciting new policy we. Have eh poem called 'Thee Road Not Taken' from thee great American poet Robin Forest." A scuffling noise, some brief urgent whispering, then the PA cuts out with a click. After a beat it pops back on. "Correction," mutters Ms. Champoux. "Thee great American poet Robert Frost."

By C Period, which is going to be geometry, Meghan feels like she's already lived a dozen exhausting lives. When she walks into Room B14 and sees that it's one of the rooms with only blue desk chairs in it, she feels her heart sink—the blue desk chairs are the narrow ones, the ones she has to wedge herself into inch by gasping inch, the ones she's been known to get stuck in once she's clamped between the seat and the wraparound desk. In the far corner of the room, partially obscured by a cluster of tanned midriffs and low-rider jeans, she spots J-Bar, wheaten head thrown back in laughter, his long, white-Nike'd feet propped up on the desk in front of him. She doesn't have it in her to perform her desk-chair comedy routine for him right now. Suddenly, desperately, she needs a break.

Ms. Flenser, the geometry teacher, new to Valley Regional this year, is standing behind her desk at the front of the room, bouncing rhythmically against it in what looks like a nervous tic.

"Will you people take your seats please so we can get started?" she barks out in the strangled voice of a seal, even though the bell won't ring for another two minutes.

In one visual gulp Meghan takes in the new math teacher: the wide, loose ass inside the too-tight pink pants, the faint mustache on her upper lip, the way she's digging the uneven nails of her right hand into the picked-raw cuticles of her left, the way the shapeless hair draped over her scalp trembles like a slab of liver every time she bounces off her desk. Okay, Ms. Flenser is an angry person. Ms. Flenser will not be spontaneously delighted to give Meghan a health pass on the first day of school.

Meghan pants a little, quietly, into the collar of her windbreaker so her skin will be sufficiently clammy and pale. She tousles her bangs discreetly, pulls some hanks of hair into her eyes. Then she assembles her most anguished migraine face, takes a deep breath, and shuffles toward Ms. Flenser's desk.

The nurse's office is a windowless cinder-block cell painted maximum-security green. It has two banks of fluorescents on its ceiling, but for as long as Meghan's been coming here the left-side bank has been out and the right side has suffered from an epileptic tremor, so the light in the room has the silty, flickering quality of a tank in a cheap roadside aquarium. The room reeks of something tangy and powdery—Ace bandages and antifungal creams—and even though it's the kind of smell that makes normal people gag, to Meghan it's the smell of relief, the smell of revelation. When she pushes open the door to the office and it hits her for the first time since June, she takes a deep drag of the stale, acrid air.

Facts about Mrs. Chuddy, School Nurse: Mrs. Chuddy is as plump and merry as a garden gnome. She is cheerful and kindly and round all over—round-cheeked, round-eyed, hugely round-boobed, her round head haloed by a spherical perm. Mrs. Chuddy only ever wears two kinds of tops: cardigans with cheerful barnyard scenes knitted into them, and sweatshirts emblazoned with cheerful, tongue-in-cheek slogans: SHE WHO MUST BE OBEYED is one of her favorites; BECAUSE I'M THE GRANDMA, THAT'S WHY! is another. Mrs. Chuddy is the most gullible person Meghan has ever encountered. Maybe it's because, even though she's a health professional, she doesn't really care about symptoms, she cares about caring. The world makes her heart break; she feels sorry for everything that lives and breathes. It's this sympathy that has made her Meghan's single most valuable source in school.

Now she hands Mrs. Chuddy her pass. Mrs. Chuddy tips the globe of her head to one side, makes a murmuring noise at the back of her throat as she copies Meghan's name onto her sign-in sheet.

"Meghan honey, so soon?" Mrs. Chuddy murmurs, peering up at her through her round, red plastic-rimmed glasses. Meghan shrugs, apologetic. "What is it, honey, a migraine?" Meghan nods. "Already? On the first day of school?" Meghan shrugs again, lets her tearful eyes drift up the wall.

Mrs. Chuddy sighs a bosomy sigh, full of pity for the great, helpless creature she sees before her. "Oh honey, I hoped I wouldn't see you around here so much this year. But it's all right, if you're sick, we'll take care of you." Bracing both puffy hands on the fake wood of her desk, Mrs. Chuddy pushes herself to her feet and scrapes back her chair with a metal squeal.

"Your usual spot?" Mrs. Chuddy asks. Meghan nods, and Mrs. Chuddy trundles toward the sickroom to pull a fresh length of wax paper over the bed closest to the door.

"Bed" is really too generous a word for this thing—it's a bench with a hard vinyl surface and a slightly raised end: the blunt idea of a pillow. Lying down on it is about as comfortable as lying down on the hood of a car. But Meghan could care less. She lies back on it now—the wax paper crackles—and lets her eyes flutter closed in a consumptive swoon. In the doorway Mrs. Chuddy sighs, *tsks* her sympathy; Meghan imagines her thinking, *Poor, poor thing.*

"Lights off?" says Mrs. Chuddy, hushed and motherly. Meghan nods, and Mrs. Chuddy flips the switch off at the exact moment that Meghan flips her eyes open to a darkness so familiar, so full of possibilities, that she can't keep a grin from breaking over her face.

Here in the dark she disappears completely, her body dissolves, but every one of her senses sharpens: vision, scent, memory, hearing.

Meghan tilts her head toward the door and curves her whole self into a listening device. She wakes up every sleeping cell in her body to listen. She makes her skin listen, she makes her eyelashes listen. She stills her breath, lets it in and out of her lungs in faint wisps. She listens so hard she feels her heartbeat slow.

After only a minute it begins. Mrs. Chuddy's phone rings—two quick bleats, an interoffice call.

"Health office?" says Mrs. Chuddy in the innocent tone she always uses when she first picks up the phone. There's a moment's pause. Then her voice drops down into its intimate range: "Yes? Oh, *yes*? Oh, Vivvie, what is it?" Score: It's Vivvie Vaughan, the guidance secretary, Mrs. Chuddy's best friend and confidante. "No," Mrs. Chuddy says reassuringly to Ms. Vaughan. "No one's here, go right ahead."

Pause while she gets the first line of the story.

"Oh, he *didn't* now! He sent a memo complaining already? On the first day of school?"

Who sent a memo complaining about what?

"I know, I thought he'd cool off over the summer."

Cool off from . . . ?

"Well if he starts rocking the boat this year he knows what's in store for him. Last year was a warning, wasn't it. With the school board and . . . Yes. Oh yes. Oh my yes. And now that Skip's given him the morning announcements thing, you know he's going to expect a little cooperation in return."

Skip is Dr. Skip Dempsey, Principal. And the boat rocker who got the morning announcements thing is . . . ?

"Well you know that I adore the man. I always have. I used to be in aquarobics with him at the Y, you remember, and we just had the best time in that class. The best exercise I ever got was the workout he gave my sides making me laugh every Wednesday. He's a peach and I want nothing but the best for him. But sometimes he doesn't know when to stop. He just pushes and pushes until people can't—"

"Hello?" From across the room, another voice.

"Oh—oh yes honey, come in!" Mrs. Chuddy murmurs something inaudible into the phone, then Meghan hears a clunk as the receiver hits home. Her jaw clenches with frustration at the interruption.

"Yes, honey? What can I help you with?"

"Yeah, I'm having an allergic reaction?"

It's a girl's voice, crisp and cool. Meghan doesn't recognize the sound—a new freshman?

"Allergic reaction? Oh, you poor thing!" Meghan hears Mrs. Chuddy get sloppily to her feet. "Did you eat a nut? Did you eat a little piece of nut by mistake?"

"No, it was soy milk."

"Soy milk? Are you sure?"

"Yes, I'm positive."

"Well I don't know, honey, I never heard of someone being allergic to soy milk before."

"Well I'm definitely having a reaction, and soy milk is the only thing I had so far today."

Something about this voice, thin as paper but sharp as a paper cut, makes Meghan want to see the girl it belongs to. Very carefully, a millimeter at a time so as not to cause a single wax-paper crackle, Meghan peels herself up off the bench to get a look at this girl. She winches the top half of her body forward until she's within viewing range of the desk outside.

The first thing is that the girl is extremely thin. She looks like a refugee from a famine-stricken nation whose American host family just bought her new clothes at the mall. Her shoulders, round and knobby, stand out like newel posts inside her black turtleneck. Her legs are as thin as arms in her jeans, and her arms are folded squarely across the empty space of her chest: the anorexic's classic posture of self-defense. On her head is a floppy black velvet hat—kind of like a cross between an Abraham Lincoln stovepipe hat and a beret—and her pinched, angry face peers out from underneath it, pressed in between two beige wedges of hair. The narrow line of her lipsticked mouth is so dark it looks black. Her pointy chin juts out at a go-ahead-make-my-day angle. She doesn't look like a girl who's having an allergic reaction. She looks like a girl who's having a fight.

"Now honey, I only want to help you feel better, but are you absolutely sure you're having an allergic reaction?"

"I think I know when I'm having an allergic reaction because it happens to me all the time, but if you're asking me for some kind of proof that I'm having one then my pulse rate is a hundred and eighty-four beats per minute and I'm hyperventilating and feeling dizzy and disoriented and I'm having trouble concentrating in class. Are you trying to say I'm making this up?"

"Of course I don't think you're making it up." Mrs. Chuddy sounds a little hurt. "I just thought that maybe you—never mind. What can I do right now to help you feel better? Do you have your epi pen with you?"

"My what?" The thin girl blinks.

"Your epi pen? To give yourself an antihistamine injection? Didn't your allergist prescribe you one?"

"Um, not yet. He's going to, though. Soon."

Obviously the thin girl has no idea what an epi pen is. Rookie mistake, Meghan thinks. Always get real meds to back up a fake illness. It can be hard to put one over on an actual doctor, but that's what makes headaches so perfect: you squint a little and you cry a little, and who can prove that you don't really have one?

"All right, honey. Well you make sure you get that prescription. Allergies are serious business—that epi pen could save your life." A mild note of superiority has crept into Mrs. Chuddy's voice; Meghan recognizes it from when she trades stories with Ms. Vaughan about Ms. Verlinsky, the slutty child development teacher. Clearly Mrs. Chuddy feels like she won this little battle.

"Okay," the thin girl says, and some of the wind has gone out of her sails.

"Would you like to lie down for the rest of the period? I've got one person in my sickroom but there's two beds in there."

"Sure," says the thin girl.

"Just tell me your name so I can check you in as present."

"Aimee Zorn," says the thin girl. "With an *i* and two *e*'s."

Park yourself, weightless, up against the sickroom ceiling. Spread yourself, formless, across the acoustic tiles. Look down in the dark at the pair of girls lying on the pair of vinyl beds. See how the thin girl curves away toward the wall, pulls the brim of her velvet hat down to cover her face. See how the fat girl stares up at the ceiling, her head roiling with silent plans. See the plans get more and more complex, more and more lushly illustrated, until they play like tiny fantasy movies on the screens of her eyes. Squint and look closely—you can see what the fat girl's imagining: the accidental run-in in the next couple of days, the gradual getting to know each other, the slow sharing of spaces, the slow sharing of secrets. Look at how her jaw hardens as she dreams this, fierce and determined: she is going to know the thin girl. The thin girl has been brought here for her. Whatever it takes, she is going to make their friendship happen.

The thin girl wraps her arms around her chest and tightens into herself like an embryo. Watch how the space between them widens and darkens.

And wait—wait for the bell to ring.

· 2 ·

"Also soy," says Aimee from the breakfast nook. "I'm putting soy on the list."

Her mother has been moving briskly around the kitchen making dinner, but she comes to a careful halt when she hears this.

"Soy?" says Aimee's mother. "What do you—?" She sighs. "Who's allergic to soy?"

Aimee shrugs. "Me, apparently. I had a wicked bad reaction to some soy milk today."

"Well I'm sorry to hear that but . . ." Her mother trails off. She's standing at the sink in her six o'clock outfit, work clothes still on but half disassembled: blouse untucked, sleeves rolled up, heels and pantyhose off, replaced by the pink plastic flip-flops she wears around the house. The outlines of morning makeup are still crusted to the edges of her features, the blackened inner corners of her eyelids, the dry, dark pink perimeter of her lips. She looks to Aimee like a stewardess at the end of an eighty-hour flight.

Her mother shakes her hands off into the sink, crosses to the table, and lowers herself into the chair next to Aimee's. She scoots her chair one precise inch closer to Aimee and takes a deep breath, the sign that she's about to start a Conversation.

"I want us to have a Conversation," she says.

"About what?" Aimee digs the sharp exclamation point of her elbow into the table, savors the zing of pain it sends up into her hand.

"Honey." Aimee gives her mother an innocent look, eyebrows raised. "Look," her mother says, a tiny bit desperately. "Obviously I want to respect your body, and its needs, and its innate, ah, wisdom, about what belongs in it and what doesn't. But I also feel like, sweetheart . . . what's left for you to eat?"

Aimee looks past her mother, out the breakfast nook window, across the sloping front yard to the cul-de-sac, the four identical condos facing their condo like mirror images. In the lawn the sprinkler pops its little reptile head up out of nowhere and starts hurling whips of water into the air. Subdivision magic.

"String cheese is left," says Aimee. "And carrots, and yogurt. And peppers and broccoli and kale. And Jell-O—is there any?"

"Jell-O?" Aimee nods. "There are three batches in the fridge," her mother says.

"Sugar-free?"

"Yes but honey—"

Aimee jumps from her chair, strides across the room, and pries open the sucked-shut door of the fridge. There they are: lime, lemon, and cherry, glowing like stoplights on the middle shelf. Their glistening surfaces ripple, underripe.

"I just made them," her mother says. "You have to give them a few hours."

"Thanks," says Aimee. She heads for the door.

"Hey hey, are we done here?" her mother asks, a tiny bit sharply. Aimee turns, gives her her blankest look.

"Aren't we?"

"Well, I was going to ask about your first day."

Aimee waits, motionless. Her mother sighs.

"How was your first day of high school?" she asks.

"Fine," Aimee says.

"Did you meet anybody new?"

Like a flash flood the image courses through Aimee's mind: the giant girl, slow as a prehistoric creature, the boys like a pack of wolves at her back, the girl's eyes behind her bangs open but seeing nothing, silvered over like the eyes of a dead fish on ice. The images are so vivid in Aimee's mind's eye that for a second she's afraid her mother's seen them, too.

"Well did you? Meet anybody new?" her mother asks again, a tiny bit hopeful. "Anybody who seems like they might turn out to be a new friend?"

"No," says Aimee. "Nobody." She turns and heads out the door.

"I'm steaming vegetables," her mother calls after her. "I'm steaming broccoli and I'm steaming kale. Are you gonna have some with me?"

"Later!" Aimee yells back, gathering speed, taking the carpeted stairs two steps at a time.

● ● ●

Upstairs, Aimee stands for a moment in the hall outside her room. She can envision every detail of what's on the other side of the closed door: bookshelf, bulletin board, bureau, bed—a family of harmless, cream-colored cartoon characters, her furniture, boring and stupid and not what she would have chosen. Almost nothing in her room is there on purpose—it's all shipwrecked stuff that ended up there by accident, as if the wave of her life broke over her bedroom and left a bunch of stuff stranded there like driftwood on a beach. Like her Breyer model horse collection, for example, which she only has because her grandmother started giving her one model horse every year on her first birthday and never stopped. And her cheesy posters of kittens that she used to think were cute, and her cheesy Victorian dolls that she can't remember how she got, and her cheesy ballet-themed bedspread . . . it's like a display room in a department store, the room of a fake girl. Sometimes Aimee imagines taking the few things she actually cares about out of that room—combat boots, a couple of skirts and shirts and hats, the sandalwood-scented candle she bought at the hippie shop, all six of her filled-up poetry note-books—and dousing the rest of her stuff with lighter fluid, tossing a lit match into the room, and slamming the door shut behind her as it bursts into a whoosh of cleansing flames.

That is never going to happen.

In the meantime, Aimee can't bring herself to reach out and open the door to that museum of randomness. She stands, frozen, not moving forward and not moving back.

At the other end of the hall from her room, the door to Bill's study stands partway open. The late-afternoon light pouring out of it is strong and unfiltered, since when Bill left he took not only all of his furniture but also the expensive wooden-slat blinds off the windows. "They're my favorite part of the room," he had explained to Aimee sheepishly when she caught him unscrewing them from the woodwork, standing on his desk in his big sock feet, curly head bent against the stuccoed ceiling.

She walks slowly toward the study now, drawn by its light like an earthling in the thrall of a downed UFO. She hasn't been in the study at all since Bill finished moving the last of his stuff out two weeks ago. When she gets to the door and pushes it all the way open, the bareness of the room hits her chest like a shove. Her insides begin to shrink, as if her heart has sprung a leak and is slowly deflating.

The big metal desk, which Bill bought off a crooked janitor for five bucks on his last day of college, is gone. The ergonomic desk chair, which he could never remember tipped back and was always spilling his coffee in, is gone. The two huge filing cabinets, which he called his "henchmen," are gone. The three framed early Springsteen posters are gone. And the books. Bill's books are gone.

Bill had had the bookshelves built into his study when he first moved in with them, back when Aimee was nine years old. She already liked him so much better than she had liked Ron or Peter or Frank or Jerry—boyfriends number one through four—that she had volunteered to help Bill unpack his twenty boxes of books and load them into the shelves the day after he moved in. The shelves were brand-new then, painted a glossy, optimistic white. "Just stick 'em in any old which way," Bill told her, handing her a short stack of novels. "I like my study to look like a dusty old bookshop you find by accident in some alley in London and then can never find again."

Out of the boxes came books of all kinds, leather-bound books and paperbacks, books with old-fashioned pictures on the covers and books with strange German titles, novels and how-to manuals, a whole box of textbooks and anthologies that he used in his Great Works of Modern Literature classes at the university. Aimee and Bill worked faster and faster, shoving books into the shelves in toppling heaps, until they got to the last few boxes, marked POETRY in big black Sharpie letters.

"Hands off!" Bill called out when Aimee reached for one of the last boxes. "Let me deal with those. I have a special way I do my poetry books."

So Aimee sat cross-legged on the brown shag carpet and watched as Bill opened his boxes of poetry, carefully peeling the packing tape off instead of gouging into it with his keys like he'd done with all the others, spreading apart the cardboard flaps of the box top with the attention and care of a priest saying Mass, then reaching in with both hands and lifting out each thin book, examining it, turning it over in his hands, laying it down flat on his desk before turning back for another. Finally he held something up for Aimee to see. It was a small, square volume, beat up and falling apart, encased in a Ziploc bag like a scientific specimen. The title, in big black letters on the cover, was *Howl*.

"You see this, Ame?" Bill asked her, dangling the book by the corner of its Ziploc in front of her upturned face. "This is a first edition of one of the greatest pieces of literature composed in the twentieth century. You ever heard of Allen Ginsberg?"

Aimee shook her head.

"You're telling me you're nine years old and you never heard of Allen Ginsberg, the greatest American poet-prophet since Walt Whitman? What has your mother been reading you, man, Dr. Seuss?"

Aimee blushed—only the night before she had reread *One Fish Two Fish Red Fish Blue Fish* to herself in bed. Sometimes she liked to reread her baby books at night—for comfort, not because she *liked* them or anything.

"Never heard of Ginsberg—that's child abuse, man," Bill said, shaking his head. "Well prepare to have your mind blown, okay? Are you ready to have your mind blown, Ame?"

Aimee nodded, openmouthed.

Bill opened the Ziploc bag and slid the battered book out onto his open palm. Gently, gently, he opened the book's cover, flipped a couple of pages in, and then read aloud in the smoky, drawling voice that Aimee would come to know as his Poetry Voice.

"I saw the best minds of my generation destroyed by madness, starving hysterical naked," Bill read, his voice thick with emotion. As he rumbled and breathed his way through the poem's first page the words fell down in glittering spirals around Aimee's ears, strange and beautiful as Christmas garlands: "angelheaded" and "illuminated" and "hallucinating" and "benzedrine" . . . After a minute of reading, Bill paused and looked up into Aimee's eyes. Unbelievably, he seemed to be about to cry. "Can you dig it, Ame?" he asked, hushed. "Can you dig it?"

Aimee had no idea what she had just heard. She had no idea what "dig it" meant. "Yes," she said. "I can dig it, Bill."

"Of course you can. You're so *down*, little Ame. You are one smart little ankle-biter." Bill put his big hand on Aimee's head then and squeezed her skull, making a smile pop out on her face. It thrilled her to the bottoms of her bare nine-year-old feet.

"Okay, man, this one goes on top of the henchmen where nothing can hurt it." Bill slid the first edition of *Howl* back into its bag and placed it on top of the filing cabinet for safekeeping. "Now help me put the rest of these in alphabetical order."

Lately Aimee's so over Ginsberg. This past summer, while things were going seriously downhill between Bill and her mom, she started arguing with him about Ginsberg at least once a day, trying to get him to see how annoying the Beats can be sometimes, how over-the-top and hysterical and embarrassing. But even when they were in the middle of some knock-down drag-out, even when Bill was yelling at Aimee that she was an ignorant philistine who didn't deserve to be allowed to read if this was how she was going to treat a saint like Allen Ginsberg, even then Aimee loved to be in this room with him. She loved standing near Bill's poetry books. She loved the pattern their colors made on the shelves, the sweet silent song of authors' names that the spines sang as she trailed her fingers over them again and again, the same lyrics every time: Ashbery. Auden. Baraka. Bishop. Bukowski. Burroughs . . . Turn the corner . . . Cummings. Dickinson. Eliot. Ginsberg. H.D. Hacker. Hass . . . Cross in front of the window . . . Kerouac. Kumin. Levertov. Lowell. Millay. Moore. O'Hara. Plath . . . And the final stretch: Pound. Sexton. Simic. Stein. Stevens. Whitman. Williams.

Aimee walks slowly around the empty study now, following the pattern in her mind, running her fingertips over imaginary bindings, humming silently along to the song of imaginary names.

Somewhere between where Rabelais and Roethke used to be, Aimee spots a pair of abandoned books at floor level, facedown on one of the lowermost shelves. A curl of hope unfolds in her chest— she imagines the phone call: "Hey, Bill, guess what I found? What if I drop by sometime and return them?" But even as she's reaching for them she can tell by their fat paperback spines, their glossy pink and purple covers, that these books never really belonged to Bill. He left them here not by accident but by design.

When she turns them over in her lap she sees she was right: *The Intimacy Workbook for Men* is the first book; *Save Your Marriage, Save Your Life* is the second. Not exactly Great Works of Modern Literature. And although she hears a voice in her head warning *don't— don't—don't*, Aimee opens *Save Your Marriage* to a random page and reads.

DOES YOUR PARTNER UNDERSTAND YOU? reads the heading at the top of the page.

Mutual Understanding is the bedrock of a solid relationship. In order for Reciprocal Love to flourish, each Partner needs to feel as if the other Partner knows how their mind works, cares about what's important to them, and accepts their quirks and foibles with a sense of humor. But Mutual Understanding doesn't just happen through magic—it takes work. Do the following exercise to find out how much Mutual Understanding you and your Partner apply to the growth of your Reciprocal Love.

Then a list of questions:

1. Do you understand your Partner better now than you did when you first met, or is your Partner as much a mystery to you as ever?

A blank line follows the question, to be filled in by the guy whose wife or girlfriend has forced him to slog through this book. Bill's handwriting is a cryptic mix of vertical and horizontal lines punctuated by sudden loops and slashes that bear no resemblance to letters; a short spool of this tangled scrawl unravels along the blank line after question 1:

As much a mystery as ever, Aimee thinks it says.

2. When you talk about things that are important to you but that you know aren't among your Partner's Primary Interests, does your Partner make you feel heard and listened to?

Not really, says the knot of ink on the line after question 2.

3. Do you make an effort to understand and appreciate your Partner's Primary Interests, even those you don't share?

The snarl of letters is longer here; Aimee stares at it until it smoothes out into words: *I would, if she had any "Primary Interests" of her own.*

A spot of blankness opens up in the center of Aimee's chest when she reads this, a little stain of nothingness. For a second she thinks she might get angry at Bill for writing something harsh like that about her mom, but then she pictures her mother's anxious face pleading with her from across the kitchen table to please just eat, please just sleep, please just be healthy, be normal, be *okay*. And Aimee thinks, no, Bill's totally right. My mother's only "Primary Interest" is making her life—our life—look presentable to the outside world. She doesn't care about heartbreak or pain—she'll do anything to get rid of pain: deny it, hide it, dress it up, ignore it. She doesn't care about the dark, ugly parts of people that make them suffer, and make them different from everyone else, and turn them into poets.

No wonder Bill had to get out of here.

From downstairs Aimee hears the faraway clink of dishes and silverware, her mother dutifully making the dinner Aimee won't eat. On the floor behind the door Bill's phone sits nestled in the carpet, its cord looped behind it like a tail.

"Yes?" is the first thing Bill says when he answers. His voice is almost unrecognizable to Aimee; it's steely and smooth, like a bank vault door—she's never heard him sound like this before. "What is it, Kath?" he asks sternly. Oh God—Bill thinks she's her mother. Freaking caller ID.

"Um. It's Aimee," says Aimee.

"Aimee." Bill pauses. Then, concerned: "*Aimee*. Is something wrong? Did something happen over there?"

Aimee says, "Um, no."

"Do you need something?"

"No."

"Everything's fine?"

"Yeah. We're totally fine over here."

"Well okay." Bill pauses again, lets out a breath, and the next time he speaks he's his loose, double-jointed self. "So okay, so what's up, Ame? Just called to say hi?"

"Well I, yeah, I wanted to tell you about something."

"Shoot."

"Today there was this—" Aimee starts, stops. "At school today I saw this thing—"

"Oh hey, that's right," Bill interrupts. "Today was your first day in the bigs. How'd it go?"

"Well there was this horrible thing that I saw."

"Oh yeah?"

"There was this, right when I got there, because I got there late because Mom had a thing with the Toyota, and right when I got there everybody was like running to homeroom and I saw these guys—like five or six guys, kind of like, chase this one girl down the hall."

Bill makes a huffing sound of disgust.

"What, like, *chase* her chase her?"

"Well, they were like, it was weird because it was all kind of slow. But they were—they were like saying stuff to her. Like I can't even tell you the things they were saying."

"Man. On the first day of school?"

"I know, right? I thought it was so, like I couldn't believe no one was making them stop."

"Nice to know you're safe in the Groves of Academe."

"Well yeah. But I think it was because, um. I think it was because she was like—" Aimee feels guilty even thinking the word. "She was like really, really. Fat."

Bill takes a second to think.

"Uh-hunh."

"Like, she was so fat, Bill."

"Uh-hunh."

"She like, she couldn't have walked through this door." Aimee looks up at the door to the study from her vantage point flat on the brown shaggy floor. "She'd have to turn sideways if she wanted to fit through this door."

"Wow. That must be really hard for her."

"Yeah, I bet."

Now that she's actually telling it, Aimee wants to describe exactly what she saw this morning, to make Bill see in his mind's eye how the girl's arms were as big around as thighs, how her hips were as wide across as a sofa, how she moved so slowly down the hall, like the float in her own torture parade, and how her whole upholstered, overstuffed body quaked with every step she took—

There's a faint buzzing noise on Bill's end of the line.

"Oh, hey, Ame? That's my doorbell, sorry."

"Do you have to get it?"

"Well, yeah."

"You have company?"

Bill breathes.

"No, it's just, it's the pizza I ordered. But listen, why don't you call me back later."

"Like at ten?"

"Well actually, why don't you call me another night."

"Like tomorrow?"

"Well I teach tomorrow. How about Thursday?"

"Um. Sure."

There's a pause.

"Write it down, Ame. Whatever you're seeing, write it down just like you see it, and then, I don't know, join the Poetry Club or something."

"There's no Poetry Club at Valley Regional High."

"Well then start one."

Aimee sighs.

"Poetry Club is for geeks."

Bill laughs his low, smoky laugh.

"Man, you slay me. You slay me, man. Take that back or I'll recite Ginsberg at you."

"You don't even understand how dumb this school is, Bill. This morning on morning announcements they said they're going to read a great American poem every day and then they go to read the first one and their idea of a great American poem is 'The Road Not—'"

The buzzer in Bill's apartment sounds again, longer.

"Sorry, Ame, hear that? I gotta run, sorry. You be strong, though, okay?"

"Okay," says Aimee.

And Bill hangs up.

Aimee puts the phone down and lies still for a moment. At the edge of her hearing a sizzling sound starts, like the distant whine of cicadas. She gets flashes, quick vivid images, of all the foods she ate today, every single bite of every single item. She can see, like she's zooming down through the lens of an electron microscope, into the inner structure of each food, the ingredients and then the cells of the ingredients and then the proteins in the cells and then the molecules in the proteins that made up each thing she put in her mouth today. Rapidly she examines the vibrating molecular structures for fractures or tumors, anything that could be triggering an allergic reaction in her body, knocking against one white blood cell and causing a chain reaction, summoning other white blood cells from every corner of her body, all of them rushing like emergency personnel to the scene of the crime, globbing up into a goopy, translucent ball around the offending molecule and making her whole body heave and writhe, blinding her and deafening her in a flood of metallic pain—is it gonna happen? Is it gonna happen?

Breathless, she staggers to her feet too fast—the gears and tendons grind and snap in her knees—and throws open the study door, gulping for air.

Her mother is hovering there in the hallway, a bathrobed ghost. As suddenly as it began, the simmering pre-reaction stops.

"I was just going to—were you calling someone?" her mother asks.

"It was Bill," Aimee says, too tired to lie.

"Oh sweetie," her mother sighs.

"So okay, good night," says Aimee.

"'Good night'? Sweetheart, it's seven o'clock. Aren't you gonna come have dinner with me?"

"I can't eat right now. I feel like I'm about to react to something," Aimee says. "Sorry."

She walks past her mother into her room and bumps the door shut behind her.

On the floor of her room, folded up on herself like a paper crane, Aimee opens her poetry notebook and tries to write it down just like she saw it. She writes *hips like a sofa* and *hands like hams* and *eyes like a dead fish's eyes.* Then she turns the page of her notebook to a blank sheet and writes

she is the garbage girl
everything she has ever eaten
is rotting inside her

Then Aimee snaps her notebook shut with a cardboard clap and climbs into bed.

• 3 •

Who is Aimee Zorn?

7:15 A.M. on the first day of the second week of school, and Meghan is taking a working vacation. Every day since the first day of school she's been back in the nurse's office, different periods every day, trying to run into her again, but Aimee Zorn hasn't shown up once. So now Meghan has to take matters into her own hands.

She's in place in front of the school, on a bench by the bus ramp, hunched over, pretending to eat breakfast. Okay, *actually* eating breakfast: frosted blueberry Pop-Tart. Bangs down, eyes up, watching. Bus 5 pulls up—no Aimee Zorn. Bus 8 pulls up—no Aimee Zorn. Bus 7, Bus 3, Bus 11, Bus 9—all Aimeeless. Bus 12 lumbers around the corner, a yellow submarine sloshing full of kids. Out they tumble, onto the pavement and up the wide walk in twos, threes, ones.

There.

Arms folded across her chest, too-light backpack flapping loose against her back, floppy hat (this one crimson) low on her head, straight black skirt down to her ankles, combat boots. Leaning forward as she walks, like she's pushing against a fierce wind. Even from twenty yards away Meghan can see the tough, no-bullshit set to her jaw, the queasy grayish tinge to her skin.

Bus 12 goes right by her house—it's the bus Meghan herself would take, if she took a bus instead of getting dropped off every day. It picks up mostly west of town: a few scattered farmhouses out in the hills, a couple of cul-de-sacs of split-levels in the middle of some cornfields, that one condo development—Riverglade Estates—on the banks of the trickly little Thorn River. Meghan's guessing River- glade, something tells her that's right, but it won't be hard to find out for sure.

Who is Aimee Zorn?

7:35 and Meghan is not in homeroom. Meghan is in Music Prac- tice Room D, the acoustic-paneled, all-but-abandoned cubbyhole off the art hall with the out-of-tune piano and the tricksy lock. The door can be opened without a key by giving it a kind of secret hand- shake—two sharp yanks on the wobbly knob—but only Meghan knows this; it's her place and hers alone. She is standing in the middle of the darkened room now, turning a slow circle. Practicing formless- ness, practicing blurring.

The bell rings for A Period and Meghan emerges, nameless now, faceless, neither absent nor present, neither in class nor skipping class. Having bypassed homeroom, she is a nonperson. She is shim- mery around the edges. She can go where ghosts go.

• • •

Who is Aimee Zorn?

8:05 and Guidance is still a madhouse the second week of school. Everybody wants to switch their photo elective to study hall, advanced Algebra II to standard Algebra II, Self-Defense to Individualized Fitness. The waiting area is a mob of kids clutching their schedules in inky triplicate, craning their necks to see Mr. Weil, who stands in the doorway to his claustrophobic little office signing off on changes, reaching over kids' heads for other kids' forms, rolling up his plaid sleeves as the room heats up. Meghan has no interest in Mr. Weil; Meghan wants what's behind Door Number 2: Ms. Pestano's desktop computer. Ms. Pestano may be the ninth-grade class counselor but she thinks of herself as an Artist, and she's managed to convince the Instructional Director that she should teach Ceramics I during A Period; at this moment she should be up to her elbows in slippery terra cotta at the far end of the art hall, leaving her office empty and unguarded. Ms. Vaughan at the reception desk has the phone clamped between her shoulder and her ear and is scribbling something down on a sticky note; as Meghan edges through the mob toward Ms. Pestano's open door, Ms. Vaughan stares right at her and doesn't even see her.

Into Ms. Pestano's office—why do guidance counselors always decorate with houseplants and tapestries?—and across the room to the desk where the computer's already on, already logged in. Meghan happens to know that the Guidance password, as of yesterday, is ACHIEVEDREAMS123, but how thoughtful of Ms. Pestano to leave it all up and ready for her.

"Z-O-R-N-space-A," and up comes the schedule in neat rows and columns. U.S. History I, World Lit I, French II—your basic ninth-grade day at school. To see is to remember for Meghan Ball—she casts her eyes over the list of classes and it instantly becomes part of the structure of her brain.

Enter to clear.

Escape to exit.

Who is Aimee Zorn?

10:40, dead center of C period, the time of day when, if she's sitting in front of J-Bar in Geometry, Meghan usually starts wishing she had never been born. But this morning is different. She is pressed into the L where cinder block meets vinyl siding, permanent building meets temporary classroom, and she is breathing in the smell of cut grass that comes billowing off the lacrosse field as Mr. Guilbault growls over it on his red monster mower.

Through the window of C25 Meghan has an unobstructed view of Aimee Zorn and the rest of the inmates of French II. In front of them Madame Mitkiewicz dances heavily at the blackboard, all beaded necklaces and stiletto heels and belted sweater dress, waving her plump, bejeweled hands in circles in front of *j'écrivais* and *j'ai écrit*. Aimee Zorn is writing something rapid and smooth, looking up periodically at Madame Mitkiewicz in a decent impression of Girl Taking Notes, but whatever it is she's actually writing has nothing to do with *imparfait* or *passé composé*. Amazing how her whole body gives off a so-freaking-bored vibe—slumped down in her seat, left arm dangling off its shoulder, head dropped like a sack of sand to one side—while down on the desk in front of her that right hand crawls steadily back and forth across the paper, ballpoint pen gripped in its mouth. As if her hand is its own creature, possessed of its own wild, urgent thoughts.

Who is Aimee Zorn?

12:20, beginning of second lunch, and no investigation, even this one, is compelling enough to induce Meghan Ball to enter the cafeteria. Amnesty International should investigate the human rights violations that get perpetrated on people in this cafeteria every day. Meghan Ball hasn't been in this cafeteria since the first day of ninth grade, and if she has anything to say about it, Meghan Ball will never enter this cafeteria, or any other cafeteria, again as long as she lives.

But on her way past the door to the lunch line, heading to the art hall, Meghan spots the crimson hat bobbing through the throng of haircuts. The hat disappears—Meghan cranes her neck—then flashes again by the art-hall door, ducks through it and out of sight. Meghan moves, invisible, around the edge of the crowd till she reaches the art-hall door, opens it in time to see—ex*cuse* me?—Aimee Zorn give the doorknob to Music Practice Room D a pair of practiced tugs. Just the right combination; this can't be the first time she's done it. The door swings open, and Aimee Zorn lets herself into Meghan's secret place.

At first Meghan feels a flash of anger: *Get your own secret place!* But then she imagines, over time, them sharing the space, learning to speak the same secret language, becoming the only two people in school who know the code of Music Practice Room D.

She edges down the deserted art hall until she's within watching range of the practice room door, positions herself at an angle to its narrow window so she can see through it without being seen. The window is so long and thin that she can only see a slice down the center of Aimee Zorn, who sits cross-legged on the dirty carpeted floor, holding a paper lunch sack in both hands. Extremely carefully, extremely painstakingly, Aimee reaches into the sack and draws out first a bright green single-serving Jell-O cup and then a tiny silver spoon.

As Meghan watches, Aimee Zorn peels the foil top off the Jell-O cup and places it, sticky side up, beside her on the floor. She peers down into the little cup, lifts the tiny spoon and, precisely as a surgeon, slips it into the green substance. As the tip of the spoon passes through the Jell-O's taut surface a slight pang seems to move through Aimee Zorn's whole body. She twists the spoon once in the center of the cup and extracts a perfect miniature spoonful of lime, so small and tightly carved it doesn't even jiggle as she brings it up carefully, carefully to her face. Aimee Zorn parts her dark, narrow lips, inserts the silver spoon into her mouth, and pulls it out slowly, her lips bared around it so that they never touch the metal, her teeth scraping the drop of green Jell-O from the spoon.

After this elaborate bite is finished, Aimee Zorn holds the spoon up in front of her eyes. She examines first one side, then the other, until she's satisfied that the instrument is perfectly clean.

Who is Aimee Zorn?

2:45, first-string buses gone for the day, jocks like jerseyed birds out on the distant playing fields, flapping back and forth in flocks. Halls empty, the long, waxy floors shining like marble in the afternoon light. Meghan is haunting the temporary hallway outside the temporary classrooms tacked on at the back of the building like an insincere apology, so cheap your footsteps on the carpeted floor sound like footsteps on a lakeside dock: hollow underneath.

Through the long, narrow window of temporary classroom D12, crisscrossed finely with safety wire, Meghan watches Aimee standing stiffly amid the girls gathering for the first literary magazine meeting of the year. You might expect literary magazine to be filled with Goth kids and weirdos, but at this school lit mag attracts the best of the good girls, awkward nerdettes who care about Emily Dickinson and dream of the day they'll get their letter from Swarthmore, girls who part their flat hair down the middle and wear their shame and shyness out where everyone can see it: in boxy pink sweatshirts and high-waisted jeans, chunky white sneakers, backpacks with first names embroidered on them in cursive (LAURIE—BECKY—ANNE MARIE). Harmless girls. National Merit Semifinalists. What could sharp-tongued Aimee Zorn, with her combat boots and her flinty eyes, possibly have in common with these kitten-girls?

Meghan watches as Aimee sinks into a chair at an empty desk, drops her head down so the velvet brim of her hat is all she shows to the world. She won't last ten minutes in there, Meghan is sure. She's more alone in that room full of pastels than she has been all day long. Meghan plans to retreat around the corner from the temporary classroom, to position herself perfectly to run into Aimee as she leaves the meeting.

Meghan's heart pounds as she imagines saying, "Hi." Imagines Aimee smiling—surprised but pleased—and saying back, "Hi."

But as Meghan watches, into the seat next to Aimee slides a long, creamy girl, a sweet concoction of freckled skin and pink halter top and red, curly hair. The girl blazes in Meghan's vision like a burn spot on a frame of film. She unfurls a creamy, freckled forearm onto Aimee Zorn's desk—pink leather watchband, pink beaded bracelets—and lets her rosy fingertips brush Aimee's black spider arm. The crimson hat pops up. Aimee's hard gaze meets the eye of the creamy girl and softens, just for an instant: opens. *No,* Meghan murmurs in her mind. *Oh no.* The creamy redhead says something to Aimee, accompanies it with a ravishing, white-and-coral smile that drenches the whole room in sweetness and light. *No,* Meghan pleads silently, *don't listen. Please don't listen to Cara Roy.*

Creamy Cara leans in to Aimee a fraction of an inch, adds something quick and clever to her last remark. A small, flattered smile detonates like a tiny bomb across the lower half of Aimee's face, then clears again quickly, like smoke.

Deep in her chest, Meghan feels her heart swerve and thump against a wall. She blinks twice, zeroes out her eyes, and goes.

• 4 •

"It is my privilege and my pleasure to call to order the first meeting of the year of the *Photon* editorial collective."

Cara Roy, founder and head facilitator of the literary magazine, looks like a Miss America contestant, dresses like the spunky heroine of a romantic comedy, and talks like the Secretary of State. She smiles out over the group of ten girls gathered in a circle in temporary classroom D12 and they beam back at her, ten moons reflecting her radiance. Cara's desk is next to Aimee's and Aimee is trying not to stare, but Cara Roy exerts an almost gravitational pull on her attention. Aimee unhooks her eyes for a moment, tries to look past Cara, to pick out titles on the bookshelves behind her red head, but finds her gaze dragged helplessly back to rest on Cara's brilliantly symmetrical face.

"We had a triumphant debut year last year—Becky and Moira and Anne Marie and Edith, you guys can vouch for this. We put out three gorgeous issues, and five pieces that were originally published in *Photon* went on to win prizes at the National High-School Literary Awards in D.C."

A ponytailed girl in a sea-foam green sundress raises her thin hand. Cara acknowledges her with a thousand watts of graciousness.

"Becky Trainer?"

"Yeah, I just want to say?" asks Becky. "That that's really all because of you, Cara?"

"Oh no, please." Cara smiles bashfully, like she's accepting an Oscar.

"No, totally, because three of those pieces that won were your poems? And it was totally your idea to bring in the photo kids, which is totally what made that last issue so great?"

"See, the thing that's so rewarding about working in a collective," Cara explains, "and I think this is really important to mention up front, so thank you, Becky, for reminding me, is that all our ideas belong to all of us. An idea might be generated by one individual, but once it's embraced by the group mind of the collective it becomes part of the, like, creative ether that we work in together, and everyone responds to it and strengthens it and ultimately owns it. So it's really impossible for any one person to take credit for any specific thing that ends up in the magazine, because we've all contributed to it by the time it gets there. Does that make sense? New people, does that make sense to you?"

The room nods in vigorous unison. Abruptly, Cara turns to Aimee, who flinches involuntarily.

"Does that make sense to you? Aimee, right?"

Aimee feels the movement of ten heads swiveling in her direction. Cara's face is a light source, blinding her. Aimee opens her suddenly leathery mouth and nothing comes out.

A furrow of concern darts Cara's forehead. "I'm sorry, is that wrong? I thought you said your name was Aimee."

Long seconds go by as Aimee works to send enough spit to her dry flap of a tongue to use it to speak. Twenty bright, questioning eyes stay focused on her, blinking, waiting.

"Aimee," she says finally, blurrily.

"Oh good, I thought so." Cara bathes Aimee in smile. "So do you get what I'm saying about the collective? Because it's really different from working on other extracurriculars, like Yearbook or something, where all the tasks are divided up completely separately."

Aimee nods. "No, yeah."

"We all work *together* on *Photon*."

"Yeah, I get it."

"Wonderful!" Cara lays her fingertips lightly on Aimee's arm, a confirmation of some kind. The touch of another human being makes Aimee shrink back inside her own skin, and she has to fight herself to keep from shaking Cara off. At last, at last, Cara lifts her hand away. "Well then guys, let's not wait another second to get started. Let's jump right in with Volume Two, Number One!"

From under her desk, Cara hauls out a burly black three-ring binder, the kind team managers use to track statistics in baseball. She whaps it open on the desk with businesslike determination, starts paging through the six-inch-thick ream of papers it contains. Around the room a current of giggly, excited murmurs travels, girls leaning their glossy heads together to confer, to anticipate, with mouselike glee.

"Editorial issues first," Cara pronounces, and the general tittering falls silent. "I suggest we have posters up around school announcing the call for submissions for the first issue by Monday, September twentieth, at the latest."

A round of nodding. Cara consults a three-month calendar print-out, pointing to dates with her pen as she speaks.

"I mean, working back from our printing date, which we figured out last year had to be November fifteenth in order to get the issue out before Thanksgiving, we want to set a deadline for submissions of, like, no later than October fifteenth, so we have at least a month to make editorial decisions and ask for rewrites if we need to and stuff, which means no later than September twentieth for the posters announcing the deadline, is that right? Does that sound right to everyone?"

A short, chubby girl with a brown bowl cut and zealous green eyes behind tortoiseshell glasses sticks her hand straight out in front of her and waves. Cara acknowledges her with a patient smile.

"Moira Dahlquist? Yes?"

"I move that we vote on making Monday, September twentieth the deadline for poster distribution," Moira enthuses, lisping her *Ss* sweetly against her teeth.

Cara grins. "Great idea. So moved. All in favor?"

Ten hands shoot up simultaneously. For a second Aimee forgets that she's not just a spectator at this event, and leaves her own hand splayed out on the desk in front of her until Cara turns to her again, face shadowed with distress.

"Aimee? You vote no on the September twentieth deadline?"

"Oh no, sorry, I—sorry." Hasty, embarrassed, Aimee hoists up her arm. Cara grins again, surveys the unbroken circle of eleven raised hands, and nods with finality.

"Good. So resolved." All eleven hands drop from the air, as if they'd been held up by the same cut string. "Okay, so September twentieth is Monday, next *Monday*, people. This poster has to be done, like, *yesterday*. So who wants to be in charge of designing it?" Cara turns her focus on a thoughtful-looking girl with a long head of straight black hair sitting directly across the circle from Aimee. "Edith Ting, you're a super talented artist. Remember, guys, what an amazing job Edith did on the cover of Volume One, Number Two last year?"

From around the circle, a chorus of cooing affirmation rises up. Across the room, Edith Ting blushes a blotchy red, looks around the floor as if she's trying to find a hole to dive into. Cara smiles down on her with affectionate reproach.

"Don't be modest, Edith, everybody knows you're an artistic genius. Don't we, guys?"

Everybody swears that they do.

Becky in the sundress sends her hand rocketing skyward.

"Yes, Becky?"

"Yeah, I nominate Edith Ting to design our call-for-submissions poster?"

"I think that's a great idea," says Cara. "So moved. All in favor?"

The door to temporary classroom D12 swings open and a short-ish man with half-glasses and a close-clipped white beard hurries in.

"Mercy!" he bleats, stopping short and pressing his palm to his chest. "What are you all doing in my temporary classroom?"

"Mr. Handsley, this is the *Photon* meeting!" Cara cries, mock shocked.

A wicked smile spreads over Mr. Handsley's elfin face. "Ah yes," he intones. "How could I forget that today was the literary coven's first meeting? You'll pardon me." He bows curtly, like a butler, and begins to back out the door.

"Mr. Handsley, wait!" Cara calls out. "New people, this is Mr. Handsley, our faculty advisor from English. Mr. Handsley, don't leave—talk to us."

"About what, dearest? Shakespeare's tragedies? Current events?"

Cara laughs and rolls her eyes. "Mr. Handsley is an indispensable part of our organization."

"It's true," Mr. Handsley says, growing serious. "Putting out a literary journal is a mercilessly dull business for which I provide indispensable comic relief."

"He's teasing," Cara explains, shaking her head at the English teacher as if he were a cute but naughty child. "Mr. Handsley does tons of important stuff for us, like liaise between the editorial collective and the school administration, and help us distribute the magazine around town once it's printed. He also has final veto power over every piece we select for publication."

"A power which I very rarely am forced to invoke, to my great regret," Mr. Handsley sighs.

"Oh and he also administers Valley Regional's Autumn Poetry Competition, which is coming up soon, and which I totally forgot we *also* need a poster for."

Cara turns back to her binder and begins flipping fervently through its pages.

"Clearly there are life-or-death decisions being made here whose outcome I cannot hope to influence. If you'll excuse me, ladies, I have some crucial top-level liaising to do." Mr. Handsley bows again. "I leave you in your facilitator's capable hands."

The door to D12 closes with a thwack behind him.

"What a silly goose he is," Cara says generously. "But everybody knows he's the best English teacher in this school. We're so lucky to have him as our advisor. Now okay, we actually have *two* posters to vote on. Who wants to be in charge of designing the one for the Autumn Poetry Competition? Yael Wexler, what about you?"

The wind pleats Aimee's skirt against her legs as she stands out in front of the school waiting for the late bus, the spiky energy of the *Photon* meeting still buzzing in her ears.

A navy blue Jeep Grand Cherokee, shiny as a torpedo and big as a snub-nosed tank, eases up alongside the sidewalk where Aimee is standing. Its windows are tinted and Aimee can't see in, but she knows who must be driving it. The car is presidential; it's sleek and serene; it's exactly the kind of car Cara Roy would drive. Aimee is suddenly very aware of her skirt gripping her legs in the wind, exposing their contours. She tries lamely to pull the fabric away from her skinniness, make it fluff out in front of her in a velvet buffer. The passenger window of the Jeep glides down and the red head of Cara Roy cranes toward her.

"Hi," Cara says calmly, expectantly.

Aimee makes an attempt to smile, but it feels like trying to set up a tent on her face, like she's struggling to assemble the smile out of rods and grommets.

"Hi," she manages scratchily.

"I just wanted to say that I'm so glad you decided to join us today. It's really important for us to have new blood in the collective, you know, to keep the sensibility of the magazine fresh."

"Oh. Sure."

"And I hope you're planning to submit something. You're a writer, right? I mean, I just assumed that you were."

You're a writer, right?

You're a writer, right?

"Yeah," Aimee says, taking herself by surprise. "I am."

Cara glows.

"I knew it! Don't tell me—poet."

Aimee blushes hot.

"Yeah."

"Oh I knew it, I totally knew it! The first second I saw you I *knew* you were a poet. That's so awesome, I'm a poet too."

"Yeah," Aimee says for the third time.

"So hey, if you're a poet you should submit to our Autumn Poetry Competition. If you win of course you get your poem published, but also you get it read aloud over the PA during morning announcements, and then Mr. Handsley sends it to this national literary competition, and if you win *that* you get to go to D.C. and go to this ceremony and meet all these amazing famous writers—I actually won last year and I got to meet Sharon Olds and Toni

Morrison. It was really cool. So you should totally submit. Put your poem in the *Photon* box on Mr. Handsley's desk in the English office and put 'Autumn Poetry Competition' on the top, like, in big letters. And I'll see you Thursday at the next meeting?"

Every word she has ever known has evaporated from Aimee's mind—all she can do is nod her head. But this time the smile leaps into her face, easy and natural, like it belongs there.

"Great! So okay, see you later!" Cara Roy waves at her from four feet away, the way little kids wave, opening and closing her hand. The passenger window zips shut and the Jeep purrs away, down the access road toward town.

In a wild delayed reaction, Aimee's arm comes suddenly loose from her side, flails in the air, waving at the back of the retreating Jeep. She feels a stab of embarrassment at her silence, at her spasticness. But a new feeling starts to melt at her center, too, dissolving slowly, warmly, into her bloodstream. It feels like sleep, it feels like sunburn. For a second Aimee thinks it might be the beginning of a new kind of reaction, but then she finally realizes what it is: happiness.

Above Aimee's head the low clouds pearl at the edges. A V of south-flying birds wipes across them and the beauty of that, a group of birds with a purpose they don't even understand cutting across a field of pearly gray clouds, suddenly makes Aimee want to cry. Her throat seizes and a wet, gurgly noise comes out of it.

Aimee breathes in and out, brings her eyes back down to ground level where things aren't quite so heartbreaking to look at. She takes in the leaves on the trees around the parking lot, notices that they have that plump, vegetable look of early fall, like ripening apples about to turn red.

She's working up the beginnings of a metaphor—leaves as apples, apples as symbols of evil and death—when across the parking lot in the thicket of woods, a flash of sky blue catches Aimee's eye, then vanishes. She leans forward slightly and peers into the stand of trees, waiting for the blue thing to reappear somewhere else—it's moving through the woods, she's suddenly sure, and just as surely she knows what the blue thing is: it's the fat girl. It's the fat girl, and she was watching me, Aimee thinks. The fat girl was watching me from across the parking lot.

A chilly squiggle of discomfort twists in Aimee's center, knocking out the warm happiness that had been brewing there. She realizes that she's had this feeling on and off all day, the feeling of being observed. But she can't tell if it's the feeling of being watched over by a guardian angel or the feeling of being spied on by a Peeping Tom.

• 5 •

The bell rings for B period and Mr. Handsley strides through the door to D12, his arms spilling over with books and papers, already barking directions.

"Page eighteen of your *Caesars*, please, children, and will the lacrosse lovelies kindly remove their baseball caps before I add them to my collection."

Behind and to the right of her, Meghan senses the sullen motion of Shane, Freedom, and J-Bar dragging their baseball caps off their heads, muttering to each other, running their hands resentfully through their flattened crew cuts. The rest of the class flips through their battered copies of *Julius Caesar* looking for page eighteen. The paperbacks they hold in their hands are dog-eared and taped up, soft and crumbly from years of use, and inscribed like commemorative plaques with the names of older siblings, older siblings' friends, infamous druggies, legendary basketball players from that one holy year when they took it all the way to state—ancestor kids. If you know how to read them, there is as much drama scribbled on the inside covers of these books as there is in the pages of *Julius Caesar*.

Facts about Mr. Handsley: He has two toy poodles, Perdita and Cymbeline, with whom he can be seen walking up and down Juniper Lane, where he lives. He is best friends with the Latin teacher, a tall, stoop-shouldered, stringy-haired specter named Ms. Werner. He once came to school in a purple velvet cape, swinging a mother-of-pearl walking stick—and not on Halloween. He is rumored to sleep in his own coffin. He got into trouble last year for assigning a play in Drama II—*Angels in America*—that the school board determined was pornographic.

Now Mr. Handsley scoots his half-glasses down to the end of his nose and tips his head back to see through them. He holds his copy of the play out in front of him and reads aloud in the plummy Masterpiece Theatre accent he always puts on for Shakespeare.

"'Let me have men about me that are fat, sleek-headed men and such as sleep a-nights. Yond Cassius has a lean and hungry look, He thinks too much; such men are dangerous.' Act one, scene two, lines one ninety-two to one ninety-five. First of all, who is speaking?"

In the desk in front of Meghan, ponytailed Becky Trainer raises her hand so urgently she lets out a faint squeak. Mr. Handsley can't conceal the weariness in his eyes as he calls on her.

"Rebecca?"

"It's Caesar? And he's talking to Mark Antony?"

"And who *are* Caesar and Mark Antony?"

Again Becky shoots up her hand, but Mr. Handsley raises one

eyebrow and prowls the room with his gaze. Meghan drops her eyes to her desk, but she's not really afraid he'll call on her; Mr. Handsley has always known better than to ask her to talk in front of the class. He never called on her even once all last year during Classics of Literature I.

"Mr. Boyd?"

Three desks to the right of Meghan, a dwarfish, red-faced kid who has been reading something concealed in his lap lurches to attention.

"Will you remind us, please, about Caesar and Marcus Antonius?"

"Caesar and Marcus Antonius?" Jonah Boyd echoes in his fluty voice, still uncracked by puberty. "Yes, Mr. Handsley, and well you should ask, because Caesar is the emperor of Rome and the title character of the play, and Marcus Antonius, also known as Mark Antony, is Caesar's close associate and the only member of his entourage who isn't plotting to kill him. They are both very significant characters."

"Fine," Mr. Handsley says, nodding.

Behind her, Meghan is aware of some subterranean fun being made of Jonah by J-Bar and his crew. It's barely audible; it's more like a change in the air currents in the room caused by the sneering looks they're exchanging.

More amazing than the Facts of Jonah Boyd's life are the Facts of his personality. If he knows the unwritten rules of school he doesn't follow them. He's shaped like a potato, four feet tall and round around like a barrel, and absolutely every time Meghan sees him in the halls he's yammering away at skinny Lucas Treischler or oily Timothy Lyme about whatever interesting lizard fact he's just learned, or which powers, exactly, a Master Wizard wields in Level

Four. As far as Meghan can tell, Jonah is unembarrassable. Even now, when anyone else would feel the viciousness rising up like swamp gas from the jocks' corner and shut the hell up, he doesn't stop babbling.

"Caesar actually knows what's going on, because the old soothsayer warned him when he said 'Beware the ides of March'! But Caesar believes that he's too powerful to be assassinated. Isn't that correct, Mr. Handsley?"

"Indeed," says Mr. Handsley.

"Hubris!" Jonah cries, waving his finger in the air like a crotchety old man complaining about the government.

"In*deed*—" Mr. Handsley says again, trying to cut him off.

"I would diagnose this as a *classic* case of hubris. A classic, *tragic* case of hubris, Mr. Handsley, that will lead to Caesar's downfall."

Behind and to the right of Meghan the stifled sneers break out into snorts. Meghan makes out Freedom's unmistakable lazy chortle. Jonah is their jester, and they're going to laugh.

"Excuse me, I don't see what's so funny," Jonah bleats, turning around in his seat and staring at the Abercrombie Adonises in the corner. Meghan tenses at the sight of Jonah gazing so frankly at J-Bar; it's a beautiful, horrible thing to see, a freakish little troll like Jonah daring to look golden J-Bar in the eye.

"All right," says Mr. Handsley from the front of the room.

Jonah balls his little fists and plants them on his fleshy hips. "All I'm doing is answering our teacher's questions. What exactly is so funny about that, boys?"

At this the dam bursts completely—the jocks can't contain themselves and explode into whooping laughter. The hilarity, the total slapstick comedy of Jonah making eye contact with them, acknowledging them, and then calling them "boys" just puts them over the edge. Of the group of them, J-Bar is the most contained, the only one not outright guffawing. He smiles but keeps his mouth closed, and he stares at Jonah levelly, eyes serious, warning him.

Even when that look is landing on someone else, even when there's no imminent danger of J-Bar turning it on her, Meghan still feels its stinging heat on her skin. Silently she wills Jonah to shut up, look away, disappear. . . .

"I don't understand you people," Jonah sniffs, turning back around in his seat and shaking his head. "You're all so mentally retarded, I can't imagine how you even manage to dress yourselves in the morning."

The class takes in its collective breath. The hilarity evaporates off the faces of the jocks. Even Becky Trainer extracts her pointy nose from her book and turns to watch the showdown.

"Excuse me?" says Freedom, suddenly serious. He pushes his desk back and gets to his feet slowly, unfurls himself into a six-foot-three-inch banner of preppy clothes and muscle.

"Jonah," Mr. Handsley says gently from the front of the room. Meghan's attention is drawn back to the teacher, who has folded his arms across his chest and is now studying Jonah closely.

"What?" says Jonah. "Why are you saying *my* name? *They're* the idiots, Mr. Handsley. They don't deserve your protection when they're making fun of other people. Don't you see them making fun of me?" He spins around again to face the jocks and waves his stubby little finger at them. "I know when you're making fun of me, you know!"

"Jonah," Mr. Handsley says again, more firmly.

"I'm not making fun of you, you tool," Freedom drawls from the back of the room. "You just called us mentally retarded idiots, you're making fun of *us*. Mr. Handsley, that kid's making fun of us."

"Both of you," Mr. Handsley says tightly. "Cut it out."

"You should send them all to the principal's office, Mr. Handsley!" Jonah cries.

"Shut up, you little faggot," Freedom sneers, low but loud enough for everyone to hear.

Mr. Handsley hurls his copy of *Julius Caesar* to the floor with a carpeted *whap* and the class starts, snaps around in their chairs to face the front of the room. Meghan holds her breath, suspended with everyone else in the sudden silence.

After a moment Mr. Handsley says quietly, "What did you just say?"

Freedom stares down at the floor, slides his big manly hands into the pockets of his chinos. For a second he looks to Meghan like an oversized kindergartner caught trying to steal someone else's lunch.

"Mr. Falcon, will you please repeat the epithet you just used to address Mr. Boyd?"

Freedom doesn't answer.

"Or perhaps you're not bright enough to remember the words you just said."

Now the whole class stops breathing. Teachers aren't supposed to call kids stupid, even kids that everybody knows are stupid.

Freedom's chiseled face burns, little muscles jumping along his jaw like plucked strings, his eyes boring deep into the carpet. Then he lifts his head and looks directly at Mr. Handsley. "I said *faggot.*"

"Out of here," Mr. Handsley hisses. Then he roars: "Go!"

With one rugby-shirted swipe of his arm Freedom sweeps up the floppy folder and battered book from the top of his desk, crosses the back of the temporary classroom in three strides, yanks open the door, ducks his curly head to clear the transom, and slams the door behind him with a muffled thud.

The class waits for a distended moment to see what will happen next.

Mr. Handsley presses his thumb and forefinger to his eyes over the tops of his half-glasses.

"Children," he says wearily after a moment. "I understand that adolescence is complicated. Physically, yes, emotionally, yes, but more than anything else adolescence is *ethically* complicated. How are we to behave? How are we to treat one another? These are big questions, perhaps the biggest of our lives, and they are questions that we must begin to confront as adolescents. And yet if we are young, and beautiful, and powerful, it's naturally tempting to forget about these questions, and to use our youth and beauty and power not for good but for evil. Evil is easy. Evil comes cheap, children."

Meghan steals a glance at J-Bar across the room. He's gazing calmly at Mr. Handsley, leaning back comfortably in his chair, his face as serene as a field of wheat.

"But," Mr. Handsley continues, "it is our highest calling as human beings to resist doing evil whenever we can, and to choose a life of integrity and good no matter what the cost. So if the *Caesar* teaches us nothing else this semester, perhaps we may profitably read it as an allegory for certain social patterns at our beloved Valley Regional. Allegory, anybody, allegory? Who's been reviewing vocab for the verbal?"

Becky Trainer's arm shoots into the air and vibrates there like a struck tuning fork.

"Rebecca," Mr. Handsley says with some tenderness, "there is no doubt in my mind that you know the meaning of this word. No one is more impressed than I with the breadth and depth of your vocabulary. But is there anyone else who'd like to offer a definition? Anyone who hasn't spoken yet today?"

Allegory, thinks Meghan. *A character or story that represents a general truth about human life. Synonym: Symbol.*

As if he has heard the voice inside her head, Mr. Handsley turns and looks Meghan square in the eye; he raises his eyebrows, wordlessly offering her the floor. As he opens his mouth to recognize her out loud, Meghan drops her chin to her chest and hunches her shoulders, trying to get as far away from Mr. Handsley's gaze as she can without leaving her seat.

Meghan feels him turn away from her.

"Anyone?" he says. "Any takers for allegory?"

The room is motionless, drained and dulled from too much drama. From her hunched-over position Meghan sees, out of the corner of her eye, Becky Trainer re-raise her hand, this time waving it back and forth in slow motion like a delirious fan at a rock concert.

"Rebecca," Mr. Handsley says finally. "Thank you for your persistence. I hereby call on you."

"Allegory!" Becky nearly explodes, ecstatic with relief at being allowed to speak at last. "Is like a symbol? A figure or a story that stands for something else? Like the Statue of Liberty is an allegory for freedom?"

"Very much so," Mr. Handsley concurs. "Thank you, Rebecca. So let's return at long last to our *Caesar*s, children. Page eighteen, exactly where we left off. As we read about the lean and hungry Cassius, and how he works his charms on the noble but malleable Brutus, think to yourselves who their corollaries might be in the endless drama that plays out around you in these halls every day."

Passing period, and Meghan is passing the door to the English office, a converted classroom crammed with the chunky green metal desks of English teachers, posters featuring has-been celebrities claiming to like to read, stacks of battered books leaning against the cinder-block walls: four hundred *Bell Jar*s, four hundred *Their Eyes Were Watching Gods*, four hundred *Catchers in the Rye*. The office is sparsely populated at this moment, only two teachers in it, square-headed Mr. Rufus hunched over his grading, frizz-headed Ms. Arnberger staring off into space.

In the corner of the room, by Mr. Handsley's desk covered in spent coffee mugs and heaps of manila folders and collapsing piles of papers, Meghan spies Aimee Zorn pulling something furtively out of her backpack, looking around her, guilty as a criminal. Aimee unfolds the piece of paper she's produced from her bag and smoothes it out on a clear spot on the desk. She finds an inbox marked PHOTON on the corner of the desk and lifts up the top couple of papers lying in it, is halfway through sliding her own paper underneath them, when the far office door opens, the one that leads to the foreign language teachers' office, and Cara Roy enters.

Aimee freezes. Cara strides toward Aimee, smiling broadly, and Aimee panics, starts to pull her paper back out of the inbox. Cara comes to stand next to Aimee and lays her hand gently on Aimee's arm, the arm that's holding the piece of paper. Meghan wants to go, but she can't stop looking, can't take her eyes off the place where Cara's touching Aimee. Aimee's eyes are locked on the place, too, quietly horrified, like there's a little fire burning on her sleeve where Cara's hand is. Cara says something to Aimee—they're too far away for Meghan to make out the words—gives Aimee a gentle, encouraging look, and Aimee nods. She's edging away from Cara even as she's nodding—Meghan sees the bend in Aimee's body, as if she's the pulled string of a bow and arrow, curved tautly away from Cara, like she might snap at any moment.

In a series of bright flashes Meghan sees how it could go between them. She'll catch Aimee, maybe, in line for the bus after school one day, or maybe she'll just wait until Cara leaves right now and snag Aimee as she comes out of the English office. Or for some reason— why?—she imagines running into Aimee in the woods out west of town near where they both live: Meghan will be sitting on the big rock by Thorn Creek where she likes to hang out, and Aimee will walk right up to Meghan, and she'll be weirdly happy to see her, like she's been looking for her, and she'll be like, "Hey," and Meghan will be like, "Hey."

Then Meghan will say, "I've been meaning to tell you something." She will say, "There's something you need to know."

Meghan the soothsayer will say, "I have to tell you about a mistake you're making."

And Aimee the Jell-O eater will say, "Tell me everything you know."

But then something shifts between Aimee and Cara. Cara says something to Aimee that makes her laugh a little, and she lifts her hand off of Aimee's arm, and Meghan watches Aimee relax, watches her slide the piece of paper all the way into the *Photon* inbox. Then Aimee looks up and makes sudden, total eye contact with Meghan, and her eyes widen and then narrow a little. Before Cara can turn and catch Meghan spying, Meghan drops her gaze to the floor and scoots down the hall like a luggage cart.

• 6 •

"This is so exciting, isn't it, guys? Our first meeting of the year with submissions!"

Cara Roy has brought snacks to the second meeting of the *Photon* editorial collective. The circle of girls nibbles daintily, like a hutchful of bunnies, on the Pepperidge Farm jam-filled cookies they helped themselves to from the little display Cara laid out on Mr. Handsley's desk: cookies fanned out on a plastic plate, a short stack of pink scallop-edged napkins on either side of the plate like a pair of spread hands, offering it.

Aimee has taken one single cookie, placed it at the edge of her desk where everyone can see it. But when she looks down at it her throat thickens with revulsion. She hasn't eaten anything since the two slices of apple she managed to swallow in front of her mother this morning, and her whole body is bright with hunger. A single crumb of Pepperidge Farm cookie on her tongue would bring on a gale-force reaction in her body when it's empty like this. When she picked it up she used a double layer of napkins—even letting the skin of her fingers come in contact with a cookie's fat-saturated surface would make the sizzle start up at the back of her neck.

Her mind returns instead, again and again, to the three carrot sticks that are waiting for her, tucked into the front pocket of her backpack in their Ziploc bag. Aimee doesn't want to eat the carrots— putting food of any kind into her body would ruin the perfect, pinging hunger she's cultivated all day long—but the carrots want her: they're humming to her from the backpack by her feet. Aimee thinks about how perfectly they're shaped, like miniature felled timber, how exactly she would be able to bite into them—five distinct times per stick—but how jagged and cold they would feel as she chewed, how their starchy taste would practically sting in her nose, how their edges would graze her soft throat going down. How having eaten them would feel like having said something terrible she could never take back.

"Okay, we had a fantastic first week for submissions," Cara enthuses. "Already we got two poems and three short stories. So like we did last year, I photocopied the submissions we got and whited out the names of the authors so the selection process will be anonymous. I'll be the only one who knows who wrote the pieces we read. Anne Marie, would you mind passing out the copies?"

Anne Marie leaps from her chair like she's spring-loaded, takes up the pile of collated submissions from Cara's desk, and starts distributing them with a waitressy smile, glossy brown curls bouncing around her head.

"Okay," says Cara, "why don't we start with the poem on the first page? Start at the very beginning, a very good place to start, right?" She smiles a goofy, self-deprecating smile. "So who wants to read this poem out loud for us?"

Aimee watches a cat's cradle of looks zing around the room, girls making little flickers of eye contact with each other, sorting out among themselves who they think wrote the poem. The only person who doesn't play, who keeps her eyes locked on her paper, is pudgy Moira Dahlquist; clearly this is Moira's poem. After a moment of silent negotiation, Becky Trainer takes control.

"I will," she says brightly.

"Great." Cara nods.

Becky holds the submissions packet up in front of her, adjusts her shoulders, and lengthens her neck before she reads:

> "*When the dawn begins to crest*
> *Like a robin's feathered breast*
> *Hallowing the sky above*
> *Like the gray wings of a dove*
> *Soon will come the bird of day*
> *To bloom like sun and fly away.*"

"Great," Cara says firmly and immediately, "great. Okay, so let's first say what we like about this poem."

Aimee looks down at the stanza parked, square as a cinder block, on the paper in front of her. She tries to figure out what exactly it is that she hates so much about this poem, why it makes her want to roll her eyes and mime sticking her finger down her throat. Is it the cheesy rhymes? Is it the fake poem-y sound of saying "soon will come the bird" instead of just saying "the bird will come soon"? Is it the fact that the last line makes no sense, or the fact that the whole thing sounds like a cheap knockoff of something out of *A Child's Garden of Verses*? In the backpack at her feet the noise from the carrot sticks rises to a soft, rhythmic thrum, like the whir of a washing machine on spin. Aimee badly wants to reach down and open the Ziploc and touch the carrots, just stroke them lightly with her fingertips—

"I have to say?" asks Becky. "That I think this poem is really great? I really like the way the author uses similes?"

"Yeah, and I really like the rhymes," offers Laurie, a girl so boring even her voice is as bland as a dairy product. "They're so nice."

Tall, wiry Yael speaks up next, talking around the pencil she's been chewing on the whole time: "I like how the poem is kind of nostalgic, you know? Like it makes me think of the Colonial American poems we read in Ms. Bradshaw's class, does anyone remember those?"

Nods and yeses from about half the circle.

"And *I* really like the way it makes me feel," says Anne Marie. "Like, hopeful about dawn, and the future, and, like . . ." She trails off. "Birds."

"Great," says Cara. "Great, I agree with all that. I think the poem is really strong. Now if we *were* going to give this writer editorial advice, what would we tell him or her?"

The room is suddenly absorbently silent, every girl peering deep into her paper. Then Aimee sees a little flash of eye contact pass between Becky and Anne Marie. Anne Marie nods a tiny nod, and Becky's hand goes up.

"Becky?"

"I think—I mean, I absolutely *love* this poem? But I think, I don't know, the last line might be a little off? I mean it fits the meter and everything really nicely, but the thing about the sun blooming? It feels like a . . ."

"Mixed metaphor," Anne Marie supplies.

"Right, like a mixed metaphor, like does the sun really bloom? I don't know. But it's really no big deal, it's not like a real criticism or anything."

"Okay, great," Cara agrees. "So if we were going to give editorial notes to this writer, we might ask him or her to take another look at the mixed metaphor in the final line." Cara is scrupulously—but effortlessly—avoiding looking at Moira as she speaks. "Great, that's so great. Guys, I think we have a winner. You're looking at our first official selection for the fall issue!"

Becky bursts into applause but falls still almost instantly when nobody joins her. Aimee sees Moira smile a small smile down into her lap.

"Okay," says Cara, "turn to page two!"

Aimee turns the page and there it is, spread out in front of her: her fat girl poem. It's so weird to see it there, this thing that was totally personal, totally hers, like a tooth in her mouth or a vein in her wrist, extracted from the privacy of her notebook and pinned out here on the page for everybody to see and peer at and judge.

The carrots begin to thump like drums at her feet, and Aimee feels a surge of electricity come off them, a staticky pulse of carrot energy that shoots out of the backpack and through her legs. A wave of goose bumps passes over her as another pulse follows, and another—Aimee needs to make the carrots shut up somehow, maybe shove the backpack away from her with her foot, or bring the Ziploc bag into her lap where she can stick it up her shirt and muffle it—

"Who wants to read our second submission out loud?"

Becky raises her hand but Cara smiles at her as sweetly as a nun.

"Becky, you're *such* a great reader, but we rely on you way too much in this group. Why don't we give you a break and let somebody else have a turn?"

Becky drops her hand and blushes all the way down into her boatneck collar.

"Moira? How about you?"

Moira nods nervously, picks up her packet in trembling hands, and begins to read, lisping:

> *"the fat girl grinds through the crowd*
> *a monstrous machine*
> *draped under the wide blue tarp of her windbreaker*
> *hidden behind her quivering curtain of hair*
> *she has thighs like a sofa*
> *hands like hams*
> *eyes like a dead fish's eyes*
> *she is the garbage girl*
> *everything she ever ate is still inside her*
> *and they can smell it on her*
> *rotting . . ."*

Something light and airy begins to swell inside Aimee as she listens to her poem being read aloud. It feels like a balloon inflating in her stomach and it makes her giddy, like she might float up off her chair if she doesn't grip the desk with both hands. Because as she listens to her poem being read aloud she can tell that it's good. Even here in this temporary classroom it's good. Even being read aloud by a girl who lisps like a cartoon puppy it's good. She did exactly what Bill said to do, she wrote it down just like she saw it, and it works. As Aimee listens to her own poem she gets a perfect picture of the fat girl walking past her in the hall; she feels the rolling thud of the fat girl's movements and sees the silvery patina over the fat girl's eyes— all of it, all of it, just like she described it.

My poem makes the fat girl come to life, Aimee thinks. My poem makes the fat girl real.

> "... *they circle her,*
> *swirling and cawing*
> *ravenous seagulls flying over a landfill*
> *scavenging for bits of her flesh*
> *as they swoop in to pluck out her decaying eyes*
> *she opens her mouth*
> *but doesn't make a sound.*"

"Great," Cara says as soon as Moira finishes, "great. So let's first say what we like about this poem."

Aimee watches the silent scramble to identify the author taking place in the eyes of the editorial collective. If she looks down she knows they'll know she wrote it, and anyway she's proud of her poem, she doesn't feel like looking down. She keeps her head up, following the looks as they swerve and skitter around the space. Across the circle she sees Cara look directly at her, a deep, thorough, penetrating look. The carrots send a single prickly shock wave through her ankles and Aimee flinches, kicks her backpack a couple inches under her chair with her heel.

After a second of silent conferral the girls seem to decide that whoever the writer is, she's not in the room. Then they let loose.

"I don't know, it's so . . . dark," Anne Marie says.

Becky cocks her head quizzically, like a spaniel, as she considers her paper.

"It's really, I mean some of the verbs are really active and everything?" Becky asks. "But the images are like, really upsetting?"

"Okay," says Cara, "but sometimes upsetting images can be the best things in a piece of writing."

"It seems kind of harsh," offers Edith in a small voice.

"Yeah, it feels a little, I don't want to say that it's *gross* . . ." begins Yael.

"Look," Moira cuts in, her usually quiet voice surprisingly shrill. "The bottom line here is that this piece is mean."

"What do you mean 'mean'?" Cara leans her chin on her hand and gives Moira her full, concerned attention.

"Well, okay, I'll just say it. We all know who this poem is about. And the writer is comparing her to, like, garbage? And saying she's rotten smelling? And the person who the poem is about doesn't get to defend herself or anything, like see, even in the poem she's silent at the end, she just stands there and lets the seagulls pick her eyes out and 'doesn't make a sound,' see what I'm saying? And if we publish this poem it's like *Photon* will be saying we *also* think that person is like a garbage dump, we *also* think that person is rotten smelling, and I don't think we should let our journal be used as a weapon that way."

The other girls in the circle nod solemnly.

"That's right," agrees Anne Marie. "That's what I meant by 'dark.' I meant 'mean.' I don't think we should be mean."

"I agree," Yael chimes in. "Personal insults aren't appropriate subject matter for *Photon*."

"I don't want to be used as a weapon," boring Laurie murmurs.

Aimee's breathing is shallow. The carrots begin emitting a tiny high-pitched whoop, like a miniature siren going off by her feet. Surely the other girls can hear it. Surely any second now she'll get up helplessly from the circle and drag her backpack to the bathroom and cram a whole carrot stick into her mouth, bite down on it and explode the beautiful hunger she's been building like a glass palace in her body all day long.

Cara nods thoughtfully. "Okay," she says, "can I just interrupt and say that I think this is a really important thing for us to talk about? Like, what are our responsibilities as an editorial collective? Do we have to agree with every opinion that's in every piece of writing we publish? I don't know, I don't know what I think about that. What do you guys think?"

"But we're not talking about some abstract opinion!" Moira blurts out before anyone else can answer. "We're talking about do we turn *Photon* into a place where you can make fun of a girl who's already completely made fun of and hated in school. And who can't defend herself. Right?" Moira looks around her for support, but now that Cara has expressed some ambivalence the other girls hold back, waiting to see what side she'll come down on.

"But the question is, I mean if we even really do believe that we know who the poem is about, do we think it's actually making fun of her?" Cara wonders.

"I think it's totally obvious that it's making fun of her," says Moira. "I mean, 'a sofa where her thighs should be'? That's exactly like calling someone 'thunder thighs,' it's no different or more poetic than that."

When she says the words "thunder thighs," two little pink blotches pop out on Moira's cheeks, and Aimee understands that chubby Moira has been on the business end of that insult more than once.

"Okay, I see your point, Moira, I completely understand what you're saying. But don't you think there's a lot of beauty in this poem? Maybe not the usual kind of beauty, but . . . kind of like an ugly beauty?"

"I don't know what 'ugly beauty' means," Moira sniffs, and folds her arms across her chest.

"Like okay, does anyone else see what I mean?" Cara turns to the group and they stare back at her warily. "Let's say you didn't go to Valley Regional and you didn't think you knew who this poem was about. Wouldn't you like a lot of things about this writing? Like look at line seven. Don't you think that's really amazing, how the writer compares the character's eyes to a dead fish's eyes? Come on, we were just saying how we liked the strong similes in the last piece and that simile is just as strong. And personally I think the fact that you knew right away who the person in the poem is shows that the writer did an amazing job of including really specific details about his or her subject matter. We always talk about how specific details are what makes good writing good, right? Don't you think that's going on here? I personally can totally see the scene this writer's describing."

"I see what you're saying, Cara," Anne Marie agrees cautiously. "This writer has a lot of good skills."

"Yeah, it's like, really vibrant?" asks Becky. "Even though it's really ugly, it's like really *clearly* ugly?"

"I like the writing in it," boring Laurie drones.

"It's an interesting topic," says Edith smally from the corner.

"Yeah, I totally agree with all that. Sometimes life is ugly and disturbing, and it takes a lot of guts to write honestly about that," Cara says simply, closing the case.

Moira looks away, defeated. Cara follows her look and softens.

"Okay, let's compromise. I really get what you're saying, Moira, and it's so great that you're making us think about this issue. The group really appreciates you taking a stand, but I think the group also really likes a lot of things about this poem, am I right? So I'm thinking, what if I go back to this writer and ask them if they have anything else on, like, a less controversial topic that they would like to submit? What about that?"

The circle goes nuts nodding—everybody wins!

Aimee tries to pick up her pencil from the desk but she can't make her fingers close—her hands and feet have gone completely numb.

The carrots now seem to be moaning softly on the floor. More than anything, more than anything else in the world, more than being a good writer or seeing Bill again or growing up and leaving this town, Aimee wants to put a carrot stick in her mouth right now. It would electrify her, it would change her, it would send feeling flooding back into her hands and feet. It's all she can think about right now. The desire for a carrot stick is as cavernous as a cathedral all around her.

"Great," says Cara with finality. "That's what I'm gonna do. Great discussion, everyone, really interesting discussion. Okay, moving on to page three?"

The wind is up outside, warm and smelling of leaves. Aimee is hunched in a shallow alcove near the line for the late bus out in front of the school, vaguely aware of the plush gray sky above her, vaguely aware of the asphalt beneath her boots, vaguely aware of the brick biting into her shoulder blades as she leans against the wall. These sensations are there but they feel like they're hovering about five feet away from her; right beside her, surrounding her like an embrace, is the pounding feeling of the carrot stick she's about to eat. She got the first stick out of the Ziploc bag and she's gripping it, pressing it against her thigh. It is going to be so incredibly good and so incredibly terrible—

"So okay, what else do you have for me?"

Cara materializes beside her, tendrils of red hair coming loose around her glistening face, clutching the *Photon* binder to her chest. As if she's been caught with an illegal substance, Aimee shoves the carrot stick into the pocket of her skirt, out of sight.

"I'm sorry about what happened in there, it must have been kind of weird and uncomfortable for you. But I know you have something else for me just as good. I'm positive of it."

"Uh . . ." Aimee says.

"Listen, they're really nice girls in the collective, I love them all, but they're sort of—God, I don't mean to be mean but they're sort of a bunch of goody-goodies, you know?"

Aimee feels a crooked smile crack across her face.

"No I mean they're nice and they're totally smart, but they play it safe, is all I'm saying."

Aimee nods.

"And I can tell that you don't play it safe. I mean, you captured something really amazing and brave about that person. Moira was right, right? We did know who that poem was about."

Aimee nods.

"I knew it, because it was so—I don't even actually know how you did it, it was just so perfect. I could totally see in my head what you were describing. And if it were up to me that poem would be in the magazine so fast. But you know, it's a collective, we have to make all our decisions as a group."

"It's fine," Aimee says finally. "I really don't care."

At this Cara's eyes narrow, just a fraction. She smiles curiously.

"Don't you?"

"I mean . . . not really. No."

"I guess I don't believe you," Cara says, a mild note of mischief in her voice. "I sort of think you're too good to not care. If you really didn't care, why did you submit in the first place?"

Aimee shrugs, opens her mouth to speak. Cara shifts her weight to lean in closer, and Aimee gets a whiff of her tangy-sweet perfume— it's Body Shop, the same kind that Bill gave her mother last Christmas and that her mother wore every day until the day Bill left. Aimee feels her brain begin to drift into a slow spiral, like a falling satellite inside her skull—how does Cara unravel her like this, every single time?

Aimee tries to talk, but she's forgotten how to speak English again; her mouth hangs open like a trapdoor.

"You're modest," Cara fills in when Aimee fails to answer her. "That's it, isn't it? No, it's really nice, it's a hallmark of true genius. True geniuses are incredibly humble people. They never want any of the glory for themselves, they just want to be brilliant and think their brilliant thoughts and make their brilliant art and be left alone to be invisible. That's you, isn't it."

"Maybe." Aimee manages a small smile. Her smile ignites Cara's pearly grin and they stand there for a second, smiling dumbly at each other.

"Come over," Cara says suddenly, brightly. She reaches out and there's her hand on Aimee's arm again, where it keeps ending up.

"Uh . . ." Aimee falters.

"Not right now, silly, not this second! Sunday! Come over Sunday to my house and we can like, have brunch and share our writing and stuff. You can bring your poems and I'll bring mine and we can read them out loud to each other!"

"I don't—" Aimee starts.

"Okay, please do not try to tell me you don't have billions of poems because you have billions of them and I just know it. In that notebook you're always carrying there must be hundreds, so don't try to pretend you don't have any poems."

"No," Aimee says, "okay."

"And you don't have to be shy about it because we'll both be sharing. And then we can give each other feedback, oh my gosh, this is going to be so much fun!"

"Awesome," Aimee says.

"Totally!" Cara opens the *Photon* binder and peels a pink Post-it off of the inside cover. "Okay, so here's my number and my address— I wrote it down for you ahead of time because I was hoping you'd say yes."

Cara hands the Post-it to Aimee. Her handwriting on it is round and careful, like the model handwriting on a third-grade penmanship worksheet.

"Cool," says Aimee.

"Perfect!" says Cara, and grins.

On the late bus, when it finally arrives, Aimee finds her favorite spot two-thirds of the way down on the left side. She sits down and shoves herself into the corner, compacts herself against the window into as small a space as she can fit herself. She slides her hand into the pocket of her skirt, as delicately as if she's playing a game of *Operation*, waiting for the electric shock to come when she touches the carrot stick. But when her fingertips brush it, it's as if someone has pulled its plug. The carrot is as cool and dull as a piece of wood.

• 7 •

"Good morning students faculty. And staff. Of Valley Regional this morning we will begin as we have been beginning. With eh short meditation period. Thee poem for thee day is by noted American poet . . ." Ms. Champoux breathes into the microphone, then inhales audibly, as if gathering strength. "Emory Dickerson. Will all students please be respectful and quiet during thee thirty-second silent meditation period after it is done Dr. Dempsey does ask."

Pop—the PA snaps off. Next to Meghan in the back row of homeroom Monica Balan is painting her nails a slutty purple. The room reeks of chemicals, and Meghan breathes through her mouth.

The PA sputters briefly again, then holds its peace.

"For the love of—" growls Mr. Cox. He shakes his pink waxy head and looks out at his homeroom for affirmation. "Takes a year to get this over with every G.D. day. I don't know whose bright idea this was, but I got athletic announcements to get through."

"Do it, Coach," J-Bar drawls from the side of the room.

"I mean, this is ridiculous," Mr. Cox rumbles, encouraged. "Whoever's bright idea this was doesn't respect the fact that I've got announcements up here. All right, listen up, people. Ears on me."

Mr. Cox holds the sheet with the athletic announcements on it up in front of his face.

"But the poem hasn't started yet, Mr. Cox," Kaitlyn Carmigan chirps from the front row. Facts about Kaitlyn Carmigan: She's the oldest of five kids, and Meghan sees her around town all the time herding the littler ones, pushing them in strollers and hauling them by the hand. She makes her boyfriend, hapless colorless sap Paul Muldoon, wear a tie when he comes to church with her and her family every Sunday. She is *still* a Girl Scout. "And plus we're supposed to observe the silent meditation period after."

"Excuse me, is this *your* class?" Mr. Cox barks. Kaitlyn flinches into the neck of her sweater like a startled turtle. "Is this you standing up here with the athletics announcements?" Mr. Cox waves his sheet of paper back and forth. Every one of his movements is stiffened by the thick layer of muscles he's wrapped in, hemming him in. "Is this you up here talking right now? No, this is me up here talking right now, which means this must be my class, I must be the teacher up here. So settle down and listen up."

Kaitlyn's nose twitches pitifully, like a bunny's, and she stares up at the ceiling to keep a baby swell of tears from overflowing the cup of her lower eyelid. Mr. Cox shakes his head.

"JV lacrosse is at home today versus Gateway," he reads grimly.

The PA crackles to life again.

"I'm nobody," whines Ms. Champoux.

"Varsity lacrosse will be away at Hamp."

"Who are you. Are you nobody too."

"JV wrestling is away at Minnechaug."

"Then there's eh pair of us don't tell."

"Varsity wrestling is at home against Auburn."

"They'd banish us you know. How—"

"Varsity girls' softball is—"

"—dreary to be—"

"—home against Whately—"

"—somebody how public—"

"—JV girls are at Sacred Heart—"

"—like eh frog—"

"—and cross country is . . . did she just say frog?"

"To tell your name thee livelong June to an admiring bog."

Ms. Champoux exhales with audible relief and the PA snaps off. Mr. Cox pushes back his chair and hoists all 250 pounds of burl to his feet.

"Okay, I'm serious, who was listening to that?" he demands, looking out at the room. "Because I think we just heard a poem about a frog during valuable morning announcement time. Am I right? Did we just hear a poem about a frog? Like in a cartoon?"

About half the class, including J-Bar, laughs lazily. Next to Meghan, Monica Balan blows across all ten of her wet purple nails.

"No, I'd honestly like to know, what the H. kind of poetry is this? While we're wasting valuable morning announcement time hearing stories about frogs, I could be telling you about things that actually affect this school, like the fact that"—he scans his announcement sheet rapidly—"uh, the FBLA fund-raising chocolate bars will be in Ms. Schwank's room for pickup after school today, and the Mock Trial scrimmage will be held at three fifteen in the cafeteria annex, and—"

Pop! The whole class winces as the PA bursts back on with a swell of feedback.

"Attention!" Ms. Champoux sounds out of breath, like she's been running. "Please (*pant, pant*) observe thirty seconds of silence (*pant, pant*) to meditate on what thee poem means to you. Dr. Dempsey asks."

"Fine," Mr. Cox growls, slapping the announcement sheet down flat on his desk and thumping back down in his chair. "If Dr. Dempsey wants meditation instead of announcements, that's what Dr. Dempsey's gonna get. G. D. poetry."

There are no words for F period, which is double today, and which is gym.

It's a fine line for Meghan between sparing Mr. Cox the pain of having to look at her and not flunking his class. She has to be present enough to pass, but not so present that he has to actually deal with her, because Mr. Cox doesn't have a clue what to do with Meghan. Her very existence embarrasses him. If she were a guy he'd probably murder her and string her big fat body up next to the basketball hoop as a warning to others about physical fitness, but since she's a girl his face just sours with disgust every time he has to lay eyes on her.

Meghan knows that Mr. Cox wishes she would disappear, and every single F period she tries in some way to make his wish come true. But today would make the fifth F period in a row that she'd have clocked with Mrs. Chuddy—five in a row is one too many; she can't miss a solid week. She has no choice but to go to gym.

The unspeakable misery of the locker room. The hiding, the hunching over, the clumsy bra tricks inside her shirt. The smell of mildew and rotten sweat, the smarm of the grimy tiles beneath her bare feet. The shame of the corner she huddles in to change, the pinch of the waistband of her hateful sweatpants from the Kmart men's big and tall section—oh, the pants, the hideous pants!

The Kmart pants are the worst part of gym, because they're so big and so violently royal blue that they break any and all invisibility spells. They're like the sheet the Scooby Doo gang throws over the transparent "ghost" to reveal him: they make Meghan *appear*. Nobody can't see these pants. If there were any other any other *any* other pants in the world she could wear to gym she would, but these are the only pants Meghan could find that both meet the phys. ed. clothing requirements and fit over her butt.

Out in the gym Meghan hovers, concealed, in the corner where the bleachers meet the gym wall. The class is sprawled across the bleachers waiting for Mr. Cox: a few little wispy-pretty girls, Lucas Treischler and Timothy Lyme off to one side in a knot of bony knees and elbows, a bunch of boring normal kids, a pair of stoner kids dressed for a Phish concert or a game of Hacky Sack.

Meghan would like to make her way up onto the bleachers, to insinuate herself into this crowd. First of all the mix of kids up there is interesting—gym class does that, throws people together who ordinarily never come within ten feet of each other—and she can see just by people's posture, the way they're huddling up with the other kids in their groups, that valuable nuggets of talk are being exchanged. The smart thing would be to just stay in the corner, close to the wall and close to the exit. But when, from only five feet away, she hears Jason Hogan, the stoner kid in the hemp hoodie with the ratty blond dreads, say to his buddy Isaac Leitch, "Dude, you are not gonna *believe* what went down last night behind the 7-Eleven," the itch to get into listening position overwhelms Meghan's sense of caution. She takes a deep breath, tries to blur herself enough to make even the Kmart pants disappear, and floats out of the corner, around to the front of the bleachers. Directly into the sightline of the class.

The very moment Meghan emerges into view, across the room the double doors of the boys' locker room swing open and the jocks emerge, moving as one: a rippling pride. They make their way in a muscular saunter toward the bleachers, sneakers squeaking authoritatively as they walk—a perfect gym sound, the sound of guys who own this floor.

It's too late to return to the corner. Turning her back is not an option, backing up is not an option. Furiously Meghan tries to evaporate into nothing at the same time as she's clambering gracelessly up onto the bleachers. Lifting her leg to clear the first row is hugely awkward—she becomes aware of her whole heaving lower half—butt, thighs, calves, feet—her focus scatters. As she sits down, hyper-carefully but still feeling the entire structure resound with the impact of her butt hitting the wood, she can feel her invisibility fray into tatters. The other kids' gazes turn to land on her one by one. They're as warm as beams of light; they heat up her skin as they fall on her; in seconds the looking starts to burn.

"Looking sexy, Butter Ball."

J-Bar has appeared behind her, leaning in to purr in her ear. He must have broken away from his herd while she was tangled up in the problem of climbing and sitting. She should never have left her corner, never have taken her eye off the room. She should never have taken her eye off J-Bar for a second.

"You look smokin' hot in those pants. Did you wear those just to turn me on?"

May the pants burst into flames. May they burn to ash. May her thighs burn with them, and her butt, and her stomach—every part of her that makes him treat her this way.

"I know you want me, it's okay to admit it. You want to sit on me and crush me, don't you? You want to hump me like a dog. A big horny Saint Bernard."

Meghan's temperature spikes and she feels the air shimmer briefly; then the whole gym goes up in a blinding white blaze. Meghan sees nothing, hears nothing anymore but the quiet, stomach-turning croon in her ear.

"Why don't you answer me when I talk to you, Butter Ball? I say all these nice things to you and you never even thank me. You playing hard to get? You want me to—"

The door to the gym office opens and Mr. Cox lumbers through it. As suddenly as he appeared, J-Bar melts off Meghan's back. She feels the light, cool air in the space where he just was. A damp breeze blows the flames out in the room all around her.

J-Bar lopes along the front edge of the bleachers, then breaks into a lean, long-limbed run and half-hurls himself up into the pack of his friends. They draw him into their midst and thump on him a little as he settles himself, grinning, onto the second bleacher row, tanned elbows on tanned knees, cued up and ready to play.

"Listen up, people!" Mr. Cox claps his huge paws as he approaches them. "Listen up and settle down!"

Mr. Cox plants himself squarely in front of them and folds his arms, clamping his clipboard to his chest inside them.

"Before we get started with activities today I wanna have a little talk with you people about something serious going on in this school."

Mr. Cox begins to pace: two steps left, rock up on his toes, two steps right, rock back on his heels . . .

"This school has a reputation you can be proud of. It's a reputation that your athletes have worked hard to earn. We had two varsity basketball players in last year's all-state game, a school record. And you remember when Valley Regional took it to state, that was an H. of a year. And you know last season we came this close to kicking Gateway's narrow butts in the semis."

J-Bar and his crew lead the class in a boisterous round of applause.

"But there are forces at work in this school, people—and I'm not gonna say who, I'm just gonna say forces—that are trying to bring down athletics at Valley Regional. It's been starting in little ways, like your poetry disrupting morning athletics announcements, or good kids, good athletes getting punished for leaving class to attend away games. But when those little things start happening, you gotta look alive, because it's a sign that the whole school is going soft. It's a sign that we're losing respect for ourselves, people!"

Again the jocks applaud. Mr. Cox presses on.

"But I'm here to tell you today I'm not going to let that happen. I'm not going to let this school go soft. I may not be able to make the rules in other teachers' classes, but when it comes to what goes down in this gym, I'm telling you, from now on, the buck stops here. No more doctor's notes. No more candy-ass excuses. You come in here *on* time, at the *beginning* of class, suited up and ready to *participate*. You hear me? You got scoliosis? Stand up straight and get in the game. You're coughing up blood? Cough it up on the court, cough it up in your pinny. I don't want to hear about it. The only thing I want to hear about in this gym from now on is how badly you want to get your hands on the ball. Is this clear? Am I making myself clear?"

A roar of approval from J-Bar's corner. Freedom and Shane pump their muscular fists in the air and lead the chant:

"Coach. Coach. Coach. Coach."

The wispy-pretty girls peer at each other with half-lowered eyelids as if to say, *Just try and take away my PMS excuse.* Lucas and Timothy swallow, Adam's apples bobbing, as panicked as kittens in a lions' den. They look like they want to grab each other's hands and huddle up for protection. Meghan breathes shallowly and stares straight forward, her mind racing to piece together a new kind of excuse—a trump card, something too horrible to debate, something even Mr. Cox has never heard before.

Mr. Cox slaps his flippers together and shouts, "All right, nice and fired up—I love it. Now let's see some hustle on this floor!"

He smiles then, Mr. Cox actually smiles, and for a split second Meghan sees, like a shaft of light falling through the crack of an open door, the man Mr. Cox probably is inside, a man who likes some things and doesn't like other things, who eats ice cream after dinner and watches *American Idol* and misses his wife, is stubbornly waiting for her to come home to him before he lets even one of his hairs grow back. But those aren't Facts, that's all just Meghan's imagination, and a nanosecond later the smile is gone and Mr. Cox's face falls back into its hulking concrete grimace.

"Line up on the blue line by height!"

Mr. Cox claps again and everybody gets to their feet and scrambles down off the bleachers.

No.

No lining up.

No picking teams.

No running in front of J-Bar.

Just. No. Way.

In the chaos of kids stumbling down off the bleachers, Meghan manages to climb down onto the floor without drawing attention to herself. She begins putting together her most pitiful migraine face ever as she moves as fast as she can toward Mr. Cox.

"Captains by me!" Mr. Cox shouts. He turns and sees Meghan approaching him. "Ball!" He yells her name, points at her with the corner of his clipboard. Her throat closes up and her heart stands still. "Nurse!" He pivots, points the clipboard at the door.

Sweet merciful God.

Without a word Meghan reverses course and makes for the door as fast her body will let her go.

The gym erupts in echoing laughter the second the locker room door closes behind her, but she's free and full of joy—let them laugh at her if they want.

The air in the hallway outside the gym is sweet and cool and fresh— almost perfumed. Meghan meanders toward Mrs. Chuddy's, savoring the lilac scent of liberation.

As she rounds the corner into the senior hall she almost collides with Aimee Zorn, who's headed in a furious hurry somewhere.

"Oh—hi," Aimee says, stopping short and jumping back. "Sorry."

Meghan doesn't move, doesn't open her mouth. *Now,* a voice inside her head says, and it's so loud, so urgent, so absolutely right. *Tell her everything she needs to know right* now, *and she won't fall for Cara's line and you'll save her from destruction and she'll be so thankful to you and she'll become your best friend and—*

"I said *sorry,*" Aimee says sharply, and Meghan realizes that she hasn't responded, she's just been standing there listening to the voice in her head. "Fine, don't say anything."

Just like that Aimee's gone, shooting like a dart from a blowgun down the hall. Meghan stands still watching her go until she turns the corner into the freshman hall a hundred yards away.

Aimee never turns back to look at her once.

• 8 •

"**A**re you sure you want me to drop you off at the end of the street?" Aimee's mother asks, pulling over to the curb and putting the Toyota in neutral. "Why don't you let me take you right up to the house?"

"Mother, no." Aimee looks hard out the window of the car, away from her mother, who clutches the steering wheel with both hands and leans forward to peer at her daughter.

"Well can I at least suggest that you take off the black lipstick?"

Aimee sighs bluntly.

"It's not black," she says. "It's Black Cherry."

"Regardless, sweetheart, I'm just thinking that as a mom, if I saw a girl walk into my house wearing that—"

"*Mother?*" Aimee turns her head sharply.

"Fine," her mother says, a tiny bit prickly. "I just think you'd make a better impression on your new friend's parents if you didn't show up looking like a trick-or-treater."

That's it—Aimee's out of the passenger seat and slamming the door of the car behind her.

"Excuse me," she hears her mother say, muffled, from inside the Toyota. The buzz of the passenger-side window as it powers down. "Ex*cuse* me," her mother calls again, and Aimee stops, turns, drops her shoulders, five feet away from the car.

"What?" Aimee demands.

"Come back here, please."

"What?" Aimee asks again, but her mother just gestures: *Come here.*

Aimee looks up at the sky and strides back to the car.

"First of all, what time do you want me to pick you up?"

"I don't know, when we're done. I'll call you when we're done."

"And second of all, you forgot your Danish."

Aimee's mother thrusts a white box of store-bought Danish rolls through the window at Aimee.

"Mom—" Aimee is desperate not to touch the box. "I told you I don't want to bring those. You know wheat's like number three on the list."

"You don't have to eat them, you don't even have to touch them, you just have to present them as a gift. It's customary when you go to someone's house for brunch to bring a little something."

"She didn't say to bring anything!"

"But you're such a polite girl you thought of it anyway," her mother says, closing the case with a no-more-arguments look.

Aimee pauses, takes the box with her left hand. The passenger window zips closed and her mother drives off without another word.

● ● ●

It's one of the first real fall days, the chilly smells of smoke and apples seeming to rise up from the earth and sift down from the sky all around her. Gray clouds, tall trees, no breeze. The whole world quiet like it's waiting for something. Aimee walks slowly down Albemarle Road, the grand avenue of big, relaxed Victorian houses that runs just down the hill from the center of town. The houses here are huge and they seem to recline on their foundations, wrap their gabled arms around screened-in porches, brick verandas, glassed-in greenhouses. The garages on this street used to be barns. The trees are as old as America, solid and soaring. Aimee thinks of her own little condo unit, the spindly saplings stuck in the ground around it, how tense the unit itself feels—three cavy rooms stacked on top of three other cavy rooms, tight and square, like it's crouched on the cul-de-sac, sulking.

As she walks, Aimee balances the box of Danish on her left palm. Inside the box the soft, gooey rolls are gummed together in a mass of bun and frosting—Aimee can see them through the little plastic window in the box top. She imagines their bready bottom, almost like flesh, seething with grease and sugar and oil, only a foil pan and a flimsy piece of cardboard away from her skin.

Cara Roy's house isn't the biggest one on Albemarle Road and it isn't the fanciest. It's big and it's fancy and it's clearly very old, but it's also modest—brown-shingled instead of patrician gray or yellow like its neighbors on either side, only one screened-in porch, and with a carport attached to one side that looks kind of cheesy, like it was tacked on around the time Bill's office was carpeted. The house is comforted on all sides by big, lush trees—maples, oaks, and elms, their leaves all starting to turn—and there's a willowy burning bush out in front on the lawn that's already a flaming red. A trail of smoke rises from the chimney of Cara's house into the Sunday morning sky.

Aimee's suddenly so nervous that she breaks into a jerky little jog, runs up the walk to the house to keep from freaking out and fleeing. She pretends her hand is someone else's hand and watches it ring Cara Roy's doorbell.

After a beat the big mahogany door swings open and there's Cara, in comfy pink PJ bottoms and a tank top, barefoot and tousle-headed and smiling her warmest smile.

"You made it!" she gushes.

"Yeah," Aimee says dumbly, and feeling the weight of something foreign on her left hand, looks down and remembers the Danish. She shoves the box forward mechanically. "Here," she says, "my mother made me."

"Oh my gosh, my favorite! That's so nice!" Cara takes the box from Aimee and gazes down at it in shocked delight as if she's just been handed the Crown Jewels. Aimee feels pins and needles start to prickle through her hand—it must have gone numb while she was holding the Danish.

"Come in, come in!" Cara steps aside and Aimee walks into the dark, light, rich, airy interior of Cara's house.

"My mom and dad are in the den," Cara explains as she leads Aimee through the cinnamon-smelling downstairs, all arches and sconces and elaborate wallpapers. "They have to read the entire *New York Times*, cover to cover, every Sunday morning or they can't function on Monday. They have a thing about it."

Cara leads Aimee to the wide, arched entryway to the living room, and Aimee beholds a scene so lovely it could be painted on a souvenir plate: a crackling fire in a ceramic-tiled fireplace, flanked on either side by a pair of deep burgundy velvet couches, in each of which reclines one of Cara's parents. Sections of newspaper are spread out all around them, cascading from the coffee table to the carpet and spread across their laps, as if they're preparing to do a messy art project.

Mr. Roy is gray-bearded and agile—he looks like he probably jogs and plays squash, he has that muscles-under-old-person-skin thing that reminds Aimee of beef jerky. His thick hair is as gray as his beard, and he's got a pair of glasses perched at the end of his nose. Actually, so does Cara's mom—they have matching nose-tip glasses. Cara's mom is also elegantly gray; her hair is piled up in a loose bun on her head, wisps of it coming out on all sides, and she has a gentle face, a children's librarian's face. Together Mr. and Mrs. Roy look perfectly matched, like two bookends or two andirons, a salt and pepper shaker pair.

Aimee thinks about her mother and Bill: loose, sloppy Bill, never standing still, always jiggling his knee or scratching his neck or bouncing on his toes, and her careful, straight-backed mother; brown, shaggy Bill and her dyed-blonde mother; grass-stained Bill and her dry-cleaned mother. She remembers the barbecue they had once at their condo, the only party Aimee remembers them ever hosting together, and how it was like the guests were on two different teams, her mother's work friends neatly dressed, standing in stiff, uncomfortable groups, chasing bits of macaroni salad around on their plates and looking the other way when one of Bill's raggedy writer friends told a dirty joke or farted or burped. You could have walked around the backyard and tagged each guest just by looking at them: *his, hers, hers, his.*

"These are my parents," Cara says. "This is my dad, Dick, he's an economics professor at the university, and this is my mom, Helen, she's an independent educational testing consultant. Guys, this is Aimee."

"Hello, Aimee," says Dick Roy.

"Hello, Aimee," says Helen Roy.

Why did she tell me what her parents do for a living? Aimee wonders. *I couldn't tell you what my mother does for a living even if I wanted to. This is my mother, Kathy, she goes to work every day at a place called Macrosystems. Her boss is named Paul. Sometimes when she comes home at night she has toner stains on her hands.*

"It's such a pleasure to meet you," Helen goes on. "Cara's told us so much about you. We hear that you're a gifted poet."

"Oh," Aimee stammers. "Oh no, not—no—"

"She's being modest," Cara interrupts. "She's totally brilliant. Aimee is the best thing to happen to *Photon* since I started it last year."

"Well it's a pleasure to have you in our home," Dick says. "I'd get up, but as you can see I'm very involved in the Style Section right now."

"Yes, it's very important to Dick that he find out which belt he should be wearing this week," Helen says, making a wry face at Aimee.

"You guys," Cara admonishes.

"But I already know which belt I'll be wearing," Helen says, "so why don't I join you girls in the kitchen and help you get something to eat?"

The Roys' kitchen is a blue-and-white paradise of country charm with a wall of windows looking out over a long, lushly landscaped backyard. Mrs. Roy moves around the kitchen with efficiency and grace, fridge to cupboard, cupboard to sink, her wrists and fingers moving delicately, as if making coffee is a choreographed dance she's practiced many times.

"Cara has been waging an ongoing lobbying campaign to get me to let her have coffee in the mornings."

"I'm sixteen years old, I'm old enough to have a little caffeine!" Cara fake-pleads.

"You're too young. Too young for coffee!" Helen Roy swats Cara's pink behind with the folded-up Week in Review.

"Mom, please." Cara meets Aimee's eye and gives her a conspiratorial look: *Moms are so silly!*

"You're my daughter and I'm not about to let you ruin your beautiful, innocent body with even the mildest mood-modifying substance. Your mother doesn't let you have coffee in the mornings, does she, Aimee?"

"No," says Aimee. She doesn't say, *One sip would probably kill me.*

"I'm glad to hear it. Coffee is for when you move out of the house or when you're eighteen, whichever comes first. I don't live with my parents anymore and I am somewhat older than eighteen, so I'm going to help myself to a second cup of coffee. What are you girls having, do you want me to make eggs? Dad's going to make pancakes later, if he can tear himself away from the Arts and Leisure."

"That's okay, Mom, look what Aimee brought!"

"Ooh!" Cara's mother coos, wide-eyed, at the box of Danish. "Honey, your favorite! Aimee, how did you know?"

Aimee watches Cara and her mom interact as if she's at a live taping of a TV show: *The Happiest Family in the World.* "Episode Six: The Happiest Family in the World Makes Brunch!"

"You girls let me know if you need anything, all right? Dad and I will be down here fighting over the crossword."

"They don't really fight," Cara explains reassuringly after her mother leaves the kitchen. "They just debate."

Aimee flashes back to the last "debate" she witnessed between her mother and Bill: Bill standing at the bottom of the stairs, her mother at the top, Bill yelling, "You're the most selfish person I've ever known in my life," her mother hurling back, "I just *want* to know where you *were* last night. You *owe* me that much!" Bill yelling, "I don't owe you a goddamned thing," and slamming out of the house.

"Let's take some food upstairs so we can start sharing our writing," Cara says eagerly, and Aimee watches Cara excise two little square hunks of Danish from the tin pan, place them on two little rosebud plates, lay a silver fork alongside each one, and tuck a little napkin under the lip of each plate. It's perfect and beautiful, like brunch in a dollhouse.

Cara's room is just as Aimee would have imagined it, if she had let herself imagine it. She stands in the middle of the room after Cara ushers her in, black boots sinking into the furry white carpet, and stares at the spun-sugar perfection all around her. The walls of Cara's room are pistachio-ice-cream green with a pattern of oak leaves and acorns stenciled in brown and red around the ceiling. The curtains are white, with matching green, brown, and red stripes at the hem. Cara doesn't even have posters on her walls, she has framed black-and-white photographs, one of a city street in the rain and one of a mountain in the desert with the moon rising over it. In her mind's eye, Aimee starts lunging around her own room, tearing down the posters of kittens in baskets, the soft-focus poster of the ballet shoe and single red rose on a satin pillow, even the genuine souvenir concert poster from the *Born to Run* tour that Bill gave her for her eleventh birthday. They're ancient history, all of them, and they all have to go.

Above Cara's white-painted desk, which is neatly arranged with stacks of books and papers and binders and a bouquet of freshly sharpened yellow pencils in a mint green mug, is a carefully organized bulletin board: along the top are three vintage travel postcards—a matching white thumbtack at each corner—of Paris, London, and Rome. In the middle is a production schedule for *Photon* and a pennant from Valley Regional High. And at the bottom is a row of medals and ribbons, at least twenty-five or thirty of them, pinned to the cork so that the ribbons overlap and the medals hang in an evenly spaced line against the green wall.

"You're not looking at the awards, are you?"

Aimee jumps—she didn't even realize Cara was watching her look around.

"Um, yeah, they're really . . ."

Cara rolls her eyes. "Whatever, I should take them down. They're mostly left over from elementary school and junior high. It's conceited to even have them up there."

"No, it's cool, it's—really impressive. I've never seen so many medals in one place before. What are they for?"

"JETS, mostly. Junior Engineering Team?" Aimee nods although she's never heard of this before. "A couple from Academic Decathlon, I don't do that anymore. A few from riding, I gave that up in eighth grade. And a few from swimming, I don't compete anymore, I just swim for fitness on the weekends with my mom. But wait, okay, this one I'm actually proud of."

Cara crosses to the bulletin board and unpins the last medal in the row, a small bronze disc on a red velvet ribbon.

"This is my National High-School Poetry Award," Cara says, cupping the medal in both hands and gazing down at it with a peculiar look on her face, almost like she's looking into the eyes of her beloved. She holds it up for Aimee to see. "It has a picture of a lyre embossed on it, see? The ancient Greek symbol for lyric."

"Wow," Aimee says.

"Feel how heavy it is?" Cara lays the medal in Aimee's hand, and it is surprisingly heavy—it's as small as a silver dollar but it weighs as much as a paperweight. "Genuine bronze," Cara explains. "Toni Morrison put it around my neck at the ceremony in D.C. It was incredible. Actually, it was the greatest moment of my life."

"Wow," Aimee says again.

"Do you want to try it on?"

"Uh . . ."

"No, come on, try it on. I'll put it on you like Toni Morrison put it on me. Bow your head."

Obediently Aimee bows her head, and Cara slips the loop around Aimee's neck. The medallion comes to rest, cool and solid, against her chest.

"How does it feel?" Cara asks, leaning in to Aimee a little, eyes wide.

"Wow," Aimee repeats for the third time.

"Isn't it incredible?"

"Yeah."

"Close your eyes."

Hesitantly Aimee closes her eyes, and Cara's hushed voice washes over her.

"Just feel it. Feel how it tugs on the back of your neck? And how it presses down on your breastbone a little, feel that? It's not like any other medal I've ever gotten. It's kind of magic—I can't describe the way it makes me feel. But *you* could, you're so good at description. And you feel it, don't you? *Don't* you, Aimee?"

Aimee opens her eyes. Cara's face is only a few inches from hers, wide open and full of wonder.

"Yes," Aimee says. "I feel it."

After a second Cara smiles ruefully and shakes her head, breaking the spell.

"Of course it's ridiculous to say that there's one best poet in the whole country and that person gets a medal." Cara reaches with both hands for the medal and lifts it off Aimee's neck. "How can there be just one best poet? I know better than to think it really means that.

It's just a recognition of my hard work and effort, and I was incredibly grateful to be lucky enough to get it." Cara re-pins the medal to the bulletin board, then turns back to Aimee and treats her to one of her gorgeous smiles. "So okay, are we ready to do some sharing?"

They settle themselves on the white rug, Aimee with her back against the bed and Cara across from her beside the desk. From inside the bottom drawer of her desk Cara retrieves a pink-canvas-covered three-ring binder with the word POETRY marked in small silver letters in the top right corner of the cover.

"I'll go first, since this was my scary little idea," Cara offers with a knowing smile. She pages through the binder for a second, then holds up her hand for Aimee to see. "Look at me, I'm shaking!" She shakes her trembling hand out from the wrist and laughs a little. "I'm so nervous, God! And I'm never nervous to share my writing. I guess it's because I admire you so much. I already know how brilliant you are."

"Please," Aimee begs, "stop saying that. I'm seriously not brilliant." She feels her cheeks get hot.

"Okay, fine, but you totally are." Cara selects a poem from the binder and removes it with a snap, holds it up with both hands in front of her. "Calm and cool," she murmurs to herself, like it's a mantra she's said many times before. "Calm and cool." She takes a breath.

"'Autumn Elegy,'" Cara reads.

> "*Trees die in a blaze of glory,*
> *but people fade away.*
> *My grandmother's face is ashen—*

gray against the white nightgown,
her hand gray against the white blanket,
her hair gray against the white pillowcase.
I walk out the nursing home door
into autumn's red,
gold,
orange,
and brown.
Even the withered leaves glow like jewels
after my grandmother's
colorless room,
decorations for
the last party
these trees will ever throw."

As soon as she's done reading, Cara looks up and scans Aimee's face for a reaction.

"Awesome," Aimee says immediately.

"God, really?" Cara's cheeks flood pink with relief.

"Seriously, awesome. Is that the poem that won you the medal?"

"Oh, no, that one was about the Holocaust. We were doing a unit on it in Euro II last year. But I don't know, I was thinking about submitting this grandma one to this year's competition. What do you think?"

"Um, yeah, it's totally great."

Cara narrows her eyes. "What? You think I should change something. What's wrong with it?"

"No, nothing's wrong with it, it's awesome! I was just . . . thinking that you might add, like, one or two more details about visiting your grandmother in the nursing home, like what else do you remember besides the gray and white colors in her room?"

At this Cara smiles. "Oh, I never actually visited my grandmother in a nursing home."

"Oh."

"I just made that up. One of my grandmothers died before I was born and the other one lives in an active seniors community in Florida, she's fine. I'm just using the nursing home as a metaphor."

"Oh. That's cool." For some reason Aimee feels mildly tricked, but she can't tell exactly why.

"It's poetry," Cara reminds her gently, noticing Aimee's altered expression. "It's art, right? As in *art*ificial? You're allowed to make things up."

"No, you totally are." Aimee nods. How dumb to feel tricked by a poem. Art as in artificial. Not everything people write is true, of course not. "Well okay, so maybe you can *make up* a couple more details about the nursing home, then. Bill always says write it down exactly like you saw it and other people will see what you saw."

"Who's Bill?"

"Bill is my . . ." Aimee trails off. Mother's most recent ex-boyfriend? Almost-but-not-quite stepfather? Long-lost best friend? Poetry guru? "Bill's a guy I know," Aimee explains finally. "He teaches poetry and he knows a ton about poetry and he, like, taught me everything I know about poetry."

"Well if he taught *you*, he must be amazing."

Aimee lets this one go without comment. "Anyway, maybe a couple more details in the nursing home part, like from the five senses?"

"Thank you, Aimee, that's an awesome suggestion." Cara nods and smiles big. "I will absolutely put a few more details in the nursing home part, from the five senses. That's going to make the piece so much stronger. See, what did I tell you—brilliant!"

Again Aimee blushes, in spite of herself.

"Okay," Cara says brightly, "your turn!"

Aimee reaches for her coat, lying in a heap beside her on the rug, and extracts from the pocket the stack of poems she brought with her, folded up into a hard square of printer paper. She unfolds them into her lap and stares down at them. It's hard to know which one to bare in front of Cara—each one is so raw and personal. Reading any one of them aloud will be like ripping off a Band-Aid and shoving the fresh wound beneath into Cara's face. And something about Cara's nursing home poem is making Aimee even more scared— there's nothing artificial in any of her poems, she's worked hard to make sure of that.

"If you're too shy to read your own piece, I'll read it for you," Cara says, and in a flash the top poem from Aimee's stack is in Cara's hands.

"Um—" Aimee reaches limply for the page but Cara lifts it up out of her reach.

"Sometimes," Cara says, looking not at Aimee but at her poem, "it can be amazing to hear what your words sound like coming out of someone else's mouth. Like when Toni Morrison read my poem at the ceremony in D.C. I felt like I was hearing things in it I didn't even know were there. So just listen to this now and see if you don't hear something new."

Cara straightens her back, shifts her butt around on the white rug until she's perfectly comfortable, and reads Aimee's poem aloud, as clearly and confidently as a radio announcer.

"Hunger is a blade that carves me
I open my arms and pull the air in
—big hug!—
then poof, right through me, nobody there.
It's only me holding myself.
My arms wrap two times
around my own ribs,
meet behind my back for a secret
handshake.
I am not what was expected.
I'm so sharp—
it's cut me now I'll cut you.
Come closer
closer
No, come closer
I'm gonna make you see what I see."

After she's done reading Cara pauses, then lets out a low, slow breath.

"Incredible," she almost whispers. Aimee's auto-blush surges back into her cheeks. "No, I can't believe—this is just like with the other poem you submitted, you have this way of making us feel things without saying hardly anything, and the way you use slang, I just *love* how you use slang, it makes your writing feel so alive. I don't know, you are just so amazing, Aimee, I don't even know how to say how amazing you are."

"*Stop* it." Aimee can hardly stand it anymore.

"I *won't* stop it until you accept that you're a genius. Look at this, look at this, in like"—Cara counts rapidly down the page—"sixteen little lines you manage to capture the entire feeling of anorexia. I know *exactly* what you're talking about here."

Aimee's breath dies in her throat.

"What do you mean, anorexia?"

Cara falters.

"Oh . . . isn't this . . . a poem about anorexia?"

"Um, I guess it's . . . a poem about being hungry? And like, angry? But it's not, I mean, it's not about an eating disorder."

"Oh, okay."

"I don't know anything about eating disorders."

"No, sure. I shouldn't have made that assumption."

The conversation sputters and coasts to a halt like a car running out of gas by the side of the road.

After a long, uncomfortable pause Cara says carefully, still looking down at the poem, "I guess the reason why I made that assumption was because *I* used to be anorexic, and the poem really captured some of the feelings I used to have when *I* was anorexic."

"When were you anorexic?" Aimee blurts out, too curious to worry about being polite.

"Junior high. Sort of seventh but mostly eighth grade."

"How did you get it?"

"Um . . ." Cara looks up at the ceiling, a delicate fissure cracking through her composure. "I guess it's sort of hard to say how I got it? I was pretty lonely then, I guess? I sort of all of a sudden didn't have any friends? I had this one person I was really close to and then like overnight we weren't friends anymore. That was hard. And also I was a real perfectionist, I was always trying to be, like, the perfect student, the perfect daughter, the perfect—" Cara sighs suddenly, sharply. "God, it's so embarrassing, it's such a cliché! My life is like every dumb eating disorder movie they show you in Health. I'm sorry, it's such a boring story."

"It's *not* boring. It's not boring to *me*." Aimee feels like she'd do anything to keep Cara talking. "Please just . . . tell me the whole story."

"Well, whatever, that's basically it. I don't even have to say any more. If you know all those other clichéd stories, you know mine."

"That's impossible," Aimee objects. "No one has your exact same experience. Every single person's story is different."

"Maybe." Cara looks at Aimee thoughtfully, as if she's letting that idea sink in. "Maybe."

"So how did you get better?"

"Well, first of all my doctor made me drink these protein shakes that were the most disgusting things in the entire world."

"What were they like?" Aimee pulls her knees in to her chest to keep herself from pitching toward Cara out of sheer curiosity.

"They're basically like if you put paste and dust in a blender with milk and chalk and then drank a huge glass of it. So, so nasty. Just thinking about them makes me want to hurl."

Aimee feels her own throat back up at the thought of being forced to drink a glass of thick, gluey liquid.

"And then my parents also made me see a therapist, which I totally hated at first. I went in there thinking that there was nothing she could tell me about myself that I didn't already know, but I ended up loving her so much. Carol. She completely changed my life. She helped me see that if you're always competing to be the best at everything then you never get to actually live your life. The only way you can have a real life is if you slow down enough to really take the world in, and, like, feel what it actually feels like and see what it actually looks like around you. And you can only do that when you realize that you're good enough just the way you are, you don't need to be constantly proving yourself or beating yourself up for how much you suck at everything. You're the perfect you in this moment. That's what Carol used to say to me all the time."

"'You're the perfect you in this moment.'"

"Yeah, isn't that awesome? It's sort of hard to remember, but it's a really important idea. I write it down on the inside of every one of my textbooks as soon as I cover them, so I can see it every time I go to study. 'I'm the perfect me in this moment.'"

Aimee nods.

"That way I don't get hung up on whether or not I'm understanding things perfectly enough when I'm reading." Aimee nods again, and Cara makes a tentative face. "Hey, um," she ventures, "can I ask a big favor? Say no if it's too weird, okay? Totally say no."

"Okay."

"Can I hold on to this poem?"

Cara holds up the hunger poem.

"Um, sure. I mean, of course."

"It's just, you already know that I'm a huge fan of your writing, but this poem in particular speaks to me so intensely, I practically feel like it was written for me. It's like you're expressing my own feelings better than I ever could. I want to read it, like, again and again, even after you're gone."

"Sure," says Aimee.

Cara looks down at Aimee's poem with the same mysterious combination of adoration and awe that she gave her own poetry medal.

"Seriously, I don't mean to be weird," she says quietly, "but your poem makes me feel like I'm not alone in the world."

"God." Aimee shakes her head. "That's like, a huge thing to say."

"Well it's a hugely awesome poem."

"You're hugely awesome to ask for it."

"You're hugely awesome to share it with me."

"Oh my God, we're both so hugely awesome!" Aimee feels the laughter bubbling up from her core. "We're the perfect us in this moment!"

The afternoon glides over them, long and cozy and gray. Cara's mom comes up to check on them and offer them pancakes, but Cara shoos her away—they're too busy to break their concentration for food.

By the end of the afternoon the sky is deep blue behind the wavy glass of the windowpanes. The lights on Cara's desk and nightstand are on, casting a golden glow over the green-and-white room, and Aimee is stretched out on her side on the white rug, boots off in a heap by the door, feet in their striped socks exposed. Cara is sprawled out in the opposite direction and the room is strewn with poetry— drifts of it, pages scattered all over the floor. Under the bed Aimee's plate of Danish lies, still untouched.

Cara has read poems about a nest of baby birds, the feeling of playing the cello, a swimming hole in New Hampshire, and hunting for Easter eggs. Aimee has read poems about pain and ugliness and despair, and also a poem about the time Bill tried to make a soufflé and ended up wrecking it so badly that he flew into a rage and threw a dozen eggs at the kitchen wall one at a time, swearing at each one.

Drunk on the elixir of sharing, Aimee has gotten looser and looser all afternoon, so that now she rolls over languidly on her back and looks up at the ceiling, as relaxed as if she were in her own room by herself.

"So which poem do you think I should submit to the competition?" Aimee asks. "The hunger one, right? That one's the best."

"Well," Cara says thoughtfully, rolling over onto her stomach to examine the hunger poem, "it's interesting, it's really interesting, because yeah, I think basically it's the best in the bunch, but you have to remember who you're dealing with here in this competition. Winning isn't always about being the best, right? It's about giving the judges what they want. And I mean, this hunger poem is incredible, you know how much I love it, it's incredible and amazing and I wish I'd written it. But think about it: girls writing about hunger and body image and stuff . . . I hate to say it but the judges are all the oldest English teachers in the school, Mr. Handsley and Mr. Rufus and those guys, and they're a bunch of old men. They don't really understand this kind of poem, or they get it but they think it's not important enough to write about. It's sexist, actually, it's really uncool that these guy teachers don't care about the things girls care about. I'm going to have a serious talk with Mr. Handsley about it. But in the meantime, you have to think about giving them something they can relate to if you want to win. And I really want you to win, because I want the whole world to know what I know about how brilliant you are." Cara rummages around in the papers on the floor, extracts a page, and hands it to Aimee. "Give them Bill. Bill's killer."

"Really?" Aimee takes the paper from Cara and looks down at the poem about Bill and the dozen eggs, as long and skinny on the page as Bill is long and skinny in life. "You really think this one's better?"

"I really think that one will *win*. You want to win, right? Anyway *I* want you to." Cara shrugs a you-just-can't-see-how-great-you-are shrug. "That's my advice. Go with Bill."

In the darkened car on the way home Aimee can't stop smiling. She puts her hand lightly to her face to feel the strange, unfamiliar shape of her grin.

"So?" her mother says, a tiny bit eagerly. "You were there all day, you must have had a good time?"

"Yeah," Aimee sighs. She's feeling so floaty and good she almost wants to lean over and put her head on her mother's shoulder. It would be extremely weird and she doesn't actually do it, but she feels like she could.

"I'm glad." Her mother looks like she's holding back a huge grin. "This girl Cara, she seems like she has real friend potential."

"Yeah." Aimee sighs again.

Her mother waits for more, then asks, "What did they serve you over there?"

"Danish," Aimee says dreamily. "Pancakes. Eggs."

"And no reactions?"

Aimee shrugs and shakes her head no. She doesn't mention that being served Danish and actually eating Danish aren't the same thing.

"Well that is just wonderful news," Aimee's mother says, a tiny bit tearful. "Honey, that's just the best news I've heard all week."

• 9 •

"I have wonderful news that I know will cause all of you to rejoice."

Mr. Handsley is standing in front of the blackboard in D12 holding an 8 x 10 manila envelope. The class blinks, groggy and unmoved.

"I have managed to secure the auditorium for the Wednesday after next during our double period, for us to act out portions of the *Caesar* for one another in full dress. By which I mean togas."

Now everybody wakes up all at once: a collective gasp, a collective groan, a swelling wave of whines and objections. Mr. Handsley's voice rises above it.

"I know, it's thrilling! You will take into your mouths the words of the Bard. You will beautify your minds by memorizing his language—by which I mean you will be off-book, you will not be performing with scripts in hand. You will work independently, in groups that I will assign, on scenes that I have chosen for you. You will labor hard and ennoble yourselves. You will be transformed from mere students into . . . thespians."

A rolling snicker from the jocks' corner. Mr. Handsley narrows his eyes.

"*Th*espians, *th*espians," he lisps at them like Sylvester the Cat, tongue stuck out exaggeratedly between his teeth. "Actors. Inheritors of the tradition of Thespis."

He holds the manila envelope up over his head.

"I have here in this envelope your assignments. On the sheet I give you, you will find your assigned scene, the role you'll be playing in it, and a list of the other members of your group. I have named the groups after exotic fruits to keep myself entertained during the assignment process. The assignments are final. No trading, bargaining, or begging."

Mr. Handsley moves out among the desks and weaves his way through them with one eyebrow raised, like a predator seeking the weakest member of the herd. After a moment he begins reaching into the envelope and dropping little folded pieces of paper onto people's desks, barely looking at them as he does it. Becky Trainer opens hers, scans it quickly, and squeals in delight, turns in her seat to wave a little birdie wave to Martha Scherpa and Kaitlyn Carmigan, sitting on the other side of the room, who beam.

As Mr. Handsley approaches the jocks' corner Meghan watches J-Bar let his hand float into the air, as effortless a gesture as untethering a balloon.

"Mr. H?" he says.

"Yes, young J-Bar?"

"I don't think we're gonna be able to do this."

"No trading, bargaining, or begging, I believe I just said."

"Yeah but me and Shane and Freedom have an in-school conditioning clinic that day. Next Wednesday?" He looks to his boys for confirmation; Shane and Freedom grunt their agreement. "Yeah, 'cause we've got our first scrimmage with Gateway that night, so Coach scheduled us for a daylong clinic during the day."

Mr. Handsley comes to an abrupt standstill in front of J-Bar, his arms folded tightly across his chest.

"During the day," he says.

"Yeah."

"On Wednesday."

"Yeah." J-Bar nods a slow up and down.

"Richard Cox is requiring you to miss a *day's* worth of class? In preparation for a *basketball* game?"

"I guess so, Mr. H. I'm really sorry, I mean, I can tell how awesome this project is gonna be, and we hate to miss it, don't we guys? But we don't have a choice. This is a team requirement."

As long as Meghan's watched J-Bar operate, she can never get used to what a clean-cut citizen he becomes whenever he talks to adults. They'd never in a million years guess by looking at his relaxed, charming face that under his PROPERTY OF VALLEY REGIONAL ATHLETICS shirt beats the heart of a serial killer.

"Well now, I hardly know what to say to this. Obviously this is unacceptable. This performance will count substantially toward your final grade, and whether or not you care about William Shakespeare, you surely care about maintaining the kind of GPA that befits a young man of your stature in this school."

"Huh. Sure, of course I do." J-Bar knits his brow with concern, pretends to be thinking hard about what Mr. Handsley just said.

"I will not excuse you from my double period to go press iron in Richard Cox's gymnasium." Meghan sees Freedom and Shane exchange glances at Mr. Handsley's off-kilter cliché. "If you miss this performance for that reason it will not count as an excused absence."

"But that's not fair," Freedom blurts out. "One teacher tells us we have to do something, then another teacher tells us we'll get in trouble if we do it, that's not fair."

J-Bar shoots Freedom a shut-up look, but it's too late.

"Fairness, Mr. Falcon," Mr. Handsley intones, gearing up for a major rant, "is a questionable standard to build your life around. It is certainly not the chief value of your hero Mr. Cox, and I venture to say that—enough, enough. I'll take this up with him. Here are your assignments"—he drops a folded piece of paper onto each of the basketball boys' desks—"and I look forward to seeing your performances next Wednesday."

Mr. Handsley continues distributing assignments, but he seems flustered and distracted—off his game.

As he approaches Meghan's desk she closes her eyes to pray: Please no, no togas, no groups, no stage, no J-Bar watching, no J-Bar pointing, mercy, mercy, have *mercy* on me.

Mr. Handsley lays a piece of paper down silently on Meghan's desk as he passes, doesn't make eye contact with her.

Meghan opens the paper and reads:

MEGHAN BALL: TECH CREW

RESPONSIBILITIES: CURTAIN, LIGHTS, PROPS

THIS IS A REAL JOB, NOT A COP-OUT!

Meghan's whole body courses with relief.

"Now!" Mr. Handsley shouts, turning on his heel to face them at the front of the room. His eyes have a wild gleam to them that Meghan has never seen before. "How, children, do you fashion a Roman toga from common household objects?"

C period. Meghan, porous and vaporous, sits in the bank of chairs outside the principal's office, pretending to be waiting for an appointment. This is normally a high-risk spot in the mornings—very busy, very exposed—but she urgently needs access to the stash of hall passes Ms. Champoux keeps under the morning announcements folder in the top left hand drawer of her desk—her supply of blanks is running dangerously low. And anyway the office is full of scattered energy; there's a fight going on in the principal's office and all the secretaries are busy trying to pretend that they're not listening to every word that's slipping out through the half-closed door.

Ms. Champoux stands, red-faced and sweating, over the Xerox machine in the corner; the phone at the reception desk goes unanswered, bleating like a lost lamb over and over: *ba-a, ba-a, ba-a* . . .

Meghan tunes her ear to the conversation taking place five feet away from her in Dr. Dempsey's office.

"—too long in this job to tolerate this kind of interference!" It's Mr. Handsley, his voice quavering with indignation.

Dr. Dempsey's low, muddled rumble, clearly trying to be soothing: "Okay, Joe, what kind of *hurm-hurm-hurm* are we talking about?"

"I had three children in my classroom last period telling me *this* man excused them from participating in our performance project. A performance project that is a requirement for my class! During school hours!"

"Now that's nuts, that's just crossed wires, or nuts." Mr. Cox, unmistakably—nice and fired up. "I don't tell my guys they're excused from anything. I tell them they need to make choices, and sometimes those choices have consequences—"

"Well *that's* the understatement of the century!" Mr. Handsley cries. "If we're teaching our children to choose volleyball over Shakespeare the consequences will be dire for our entire society!"

"Now, Joe," Dr. Dempsey murmurs. "*Hurm-hurm-hurm.*"

"It's basketball, by the way," snaps Mr. Cox.

"All right, both of you, let's *hurm-hurm* a second."

"What I want from you, Skip," Mr. Handsley says, addressing the principal, "is an assurance that I may visit upon any student who misses the performance in order to prepare for the 'scrimmage'"—he pronounces the word like it's dirty—"the kind of grade penalty he or she will deserve. Which may ultimately disqualify him or her from participating in varsity athletics, I can't make any guarantees."

"Skip?" Mr. Cox demands. "Do you hear this? This is what I've been talking about, this is a vendetta! This guy has a vendetta against my team!"

"Okay, Rich, calm down—" Dr. Dempsey begins, but Mr. Handsley talks over him, clipped and contained.

"I have no such thing. On the contrary, I've done everything in my power to help the members of your team keep from falling behind in my classes. I want all my students to succeed, and I help every one of them to the degree that they need it. But the attitude of your 'guys,' Rich, is rank. It's repellent. No matter how much extra attention I give them, they regularly repay me by failing to complete assignments, skipping class to attend scrimmages and games, even taunting and ganging up on other students during class time. I don't know what kind of philosophy you're drilling them in, but to me at least it seems deeply flawed."

"We went twenty and three last year," Mr. Cox drawls. "I guess I'm doing something right."

A silence.

"Of course you must do what you believe is best." Mr. Handsley's voice is low and controlled now. "And so must I. I will not be excusing a single one of your players from our performance project next Wednesday."

"Skip!" Mr. Cox yells.

"Joe," says Dr. Dempsey, "I think we can all *hurm-hurm* your *hurm-hurm*. But we've got to keep in mind what basketball *hurm*."

"Ambassadors," Mr. Cox chimes in. "Tell him the thing you said to me about how my guys are ambassadors for the entire school."

"Please," Mr. Handsley says briskly. "I do not require a lecture on school spirit or the salutary effects of winning sports championships. I know that basketball is important to this school. But Shakespeare is important to life. I've said this before and I'll say it again now: If you teach these young men that Shakespeare isn't important, that studying and learning don't matter as much as charging up and down a painted court like a herd of animals, what you're really teaching them is that this, right now, is the pinnacle of their lives. This moment, when they're the strongest and fastest they'll ever be and have the most raw power over other people, is their brightest moment. You're teaching them that now is their real life. When as a matter of fact their lives begin when we're *done* with them, their lives begin the day they leave us behind. What do you want them to leave us with? Nostalgia for a triumphant away game at Hamp? Bitter memories of the tragic fall to Gateway Regional?"

"Now that game was rigged! That ref was a—"

"*Rich?*" Dr. Dempsey cuts Mr. Cox off sharply.

"I will not be moved," says Mr. Handsley.

"Goddamnit!" yells Mr. Cox.

"Volume, Rich!" Dr. Dempsey barks.

The door slams shut, shoved closed from the inside, and the argument blurs into murmur. Meghan watches the secretaries turn to look at each other, then move as a group to cluster around Ms. Champoux at the Xerox machine. They whisper together as excitedly as a group of ninth-grade girls gossiping in the freshman hallway.

Silently, invisibly, completely unnoticed, Meghan gets up from her seat and moves in a single fluid arc across the office. She floats past Ms. Champoux's desk, bending slightly to hoist and glide the left hand drawer open with a practiced flick of her wrist so it doesn't catch or squeal on the sticky halfway spot, dipping her hand into the drawer and under the manila folder where the announcements are kept, pinching an inch-thick stack of pink passes from their hiding place, and slipping them effortlessly into her pocket. Silently, invisibly, completely unnoticed, Meghan slides the drawer to Ms. Champoux's desk shut, slips around the reception desk, and vanishes out the office door.

D period. Somewhere else in the labyrinth of the school, Social Studies is happening—American History I: Puritans are thatching roofs and striking soon-to-be-broken bargains with Native Americans—but Meghan is in the heart of the maze, floating, a dreamy minotaur, in the dark of the sick room. She feels expansive and unearthly, like a mist, pixilated into pure hearing, distributed everywhere in the murky room at once. All around her, the soothing rise and fall of Mrs. Chuddy's information.

"I know. Well Rich thinks he's doing it on purpose. Rich says Joe singles out his boys to punish just because they're athletes, and if that's true I tell you it breaks my heart. Innocent children shouldn't be punished for no reason."

A tiny pause while she lets Vivvie get a one-syllable word in edgewise.

"Yes but I heard Rich telling Deborah in the hall, I heard him say 'Joe's trying to destroy the basketball team. Joe's got it in for the basketball team,' he said. Well I don't know why he'd do a thing like that, they're good boys. They bring a lot of pride to this school. Those are the kind of boys you read about later, the ones who turn up in the paper ten years from now doing something interesting in New York or Washington. I hate to think of all that promise getting crushed because of something Joe's doing out of spite."

Pause.

"Of course it's spite, what else could it be? Rich is just going up up up around here, Deborah said he's gunning for a regional job soon and he's laying the foundation right now, and Joe is . . . well you know I adore that man, I just think he's the best and the sweetest, and I don't like to say about someone that he's on the decline, but . . ."

In the dark Meghan imagines a thin sparkling thread running from her finger out the door of the sick room, through Mrs. Chuddy's office, out into the hall, winding through the corridors of Valley Regional, through the door of room A34 where Aimee is sitting in Algebra II. Meghan imagines the thread wrapped around Aimee's narrow ankle. She imagines tugging on the thread to get Aimee's attention, imagines Aimee's head snapping up, her hand going up automatically to ask for a pass. She imagines Aimee following the thread back through the halls, hand over hand, all the way up to Mrs. Chuddy's door. *She could be coming through the door right now,* Meghan thinks. *Now. Or now. Any second now.*

"He was never like this in aquarobics," Mrs. Chuddy sighs. "We used to have just the most fun in that class. I tell you, that man can be a hoot and a holler when he wants to be."

Meghan hears the clock on Mrs. Chuddy's wall hiccup back a minute, then click forward two minutes. D period is draining away, and still no Aimee.

Tug—Meghan plucks the thread again in her mind.

"When a fellow like that starts to lose his shine, why that's a hard thing to watch."

Tug—Meghan plucks the thread a little harder.

"If it were up to me, children wouldn't even get grades. Each child would get their own chance to shine."

Tug, tug, tug.

Nothing. Aimee's not answering.

Meghan's waited long enough. She's going to have to go directly to the source.

• 10 •

Bus 12 passes two beautiful sights on its route from Valley Regional out west of town. Aimee waits for the two beautiful sights every morning and every afternoon, checks them off in her head as they pass. She's waiting for the first one to come around the bend now, on her way home through the glassy blue-and-gold fall afternoon.

Bus 12 is a hard place to relax. It smells like eraser shavings and throw-up; the edge of the hard vinyl seat bites Aimee's legs. Sometimes if she looks up at the ceiling she gets the feeling that it's the inside of a metal coffin lid clamped down over all of them, burying them alive. But when she passes her two beautiful sights and acknowledges them solemnly, Aimee feels the spring at her center untwist a little.

The bus comes around the corner onto Hamilton Street and approaches the first beautiful sight—a white farmhouse sitting flat on a wide green lawn, no visible foundation, with a low, open porch wrapping all the way around it, and on the porch thirty forest-green plastic chairs lined up one right next to the other with their backs against the house, facing out as if waiting for thirty strangers to come sit in them and stare out, not speaking to each other, at the road. The thirty empty chairs on this farmhouse porch are silly and sad and perfect and wrong—they whiz past Aimee now on the left and she inclines her head slightly-slightly, presses her forehead against the bus window, acknowledging them.

The second beautiful sight isn't until right before the turnoff to Riverglade Estates, easily four or five minutes from now. Aimee has time to zone out a little. She lets her head jostle against the window, bonking gently against the cool Plexiglas with every bounce of the bus over the frost heaves in the road, feeling her mind drift out and over the lines of the poem she submitted to the competition. As she works the poem over in her mind she starts to panic—whatever Cara might have thought about how great it was, she should never have submitted something so unfinished. She should never let strangers see anything she's written before she's gotten feedback from Bill about it.

All at once Aimee has a vision of how this afternoon would go if it were going to be a good, normal afternoon instead of the sucky, empty afternoon it's actually going to be: she'd get off the bus at the bottom of her cul-de-sac, walk up the little hill to the roundabout, head up the leftmost driveway to the mustard-yellow detached condo unit she calls home, open the side door, yell, *Hey, it's me!* into the mud room as she dropped her backpack onto the tile floor, and she'd hear Bill's voice answer from his study upstairs, muffled by doors and ceilings and carpets: *Who's me?* And she'd yell, *It's Ed McMahon from Publishers Clearinghouse, you just won a million dollars!* or she'd yell, *It's Rent-a-Center, I've got that new carpet steamer you ordered!* or she'd yell, *It's me, Daffodil, your long-lost love child from Wood-stock!* and Bill would wait a second, like he was thinking it over, and then he'd yell back, *Cool, be right down!* And she'd schlump into the kitchen and kick her boots off into the corner and go to the fridge and get out the bowl of lime sugar-free Jell-O that would be waiting for her there, and she'd cross to the silverware drawer and take out the tiny silver spoon that's her favorite utensil, the one with Winnie-the-Pooh molded into the handle that her mother used to feed her with when she was a baby, and she'd plunk down in a chair at the kitchen table with her spoon and her Jell-O and Bill would come shuffling into the room looking all distracted and tousled, like he'd just been woken up from a nap—when in fact he'd probably been grading bad papers all afternoon—and he'd say, *So where's Daffodil?* or he'd say, *Where's my million dollars, man?* and she'd say, *I don't know, I guess she left,* or she'd say, *I guess they got sick of waiting and went next door to give the money to the Waynes.* And his shoulders would droop and he'd let out a groan and collapse into the chair next to hers, prop one of his long, skinny, hairy legs up on the table (something he never did when her mother was home), and he'd say, *Close, but no cigar. Story of my life, man.* And she'd shake her head sympathetically at him and slide her bowl of glistening green cool-ness an inch or two in his direction and say, *Jell-O? Make you feel better,* and he'd say, *Sheesh, Ame, don't you know that stuff is gonna kill you? That artificial sweetener has been proven to give tumors to rats,* and she'd say, *Whatever, Bill, I'm not a rat.* Then she'd say, *Hey Bill, would you look at this thing I wrote?*

Aimee is so engrossed in her dream afternoon that she almost misses beautiful sight number two. Suddenly there it is, passing her on the left, and she jumps out of her reverie into the real world—oh, it's so beautiful, this dilapidated gray-brown barn, maybe fifty years old, maybe a hundred, as long and narrow as a city block and silvered by decades of weather and neglect, roof caved in at the center, sides bowing out, like a lame horse that's fallen onto one knee—or no, like a ship sinking into a sea of dirt, its bow and stern still pointing up but its deck getting slowly sucked under the waves.

Aimee presses her forehead against the window to acknowledge the barn as it speeds past, apologizes to it silently for almost missing it. Then she thinks, Okay, I am officially losing it. I just apologized to a barn.

Bus 12 sheds Aimee onto the grassy curb at the bottom of her cul-de-sac and grinds away, leaving a dirty puff of diesel smoke in the air behind it. Aimee looks up the little hill to the roundabout, to the detached mustard-yellow condo unit that will answer her with nothing but a gulp of silence when she opens the side door and tells it she's home. She feels the twinge in her stomach, hears the tinselly sizzle that tells her there's a reaction coming, still out there some-where on the horizon but heading her way. Aimee imagines suc-cumbing to the reaction right here, right here in the unmowed grass by the storm drain, imagines her mother finding her—a heap of barely breathing laundry—three hours from now as she drives home in the Toyota. Imagines the Toyota screeching to a halt, her mother bursting out, leaving the driver's-side door open as she rushes to the side of the road, crying, *No, sweetie, no—*

Up the hill, something sky blue emerges from behind her mustard-yellow garage. Something sky blue and bulky; it moves slowly, takes up a place in Aimee's driveway and stands there like a giant Rubbermaid trash can, facing her.

The prereaction twinge snaps off in Aimee's stomach. She begins to stride up the hill toward the fat girl.

The fat girl holds her ground as Aimee approaches, doesn't move a muscle. Aimee gets to the top of the little hill and stops for a second, folds her arms across her chest, fixes her gaze on the fat girl's face, half-hidden by the dingy veil of her hair. A warm September breeze moves past them both, eddying Aimee's skirt around her ankles and lifting the fat girl's frondy bangs—Aimee catches a glimpse of those silvery eyes, staring directly at her, not blinking—then dropping the hair back onto the fat girl's forehead, re-veiling her. They are about fifteen yards apart, nothing but lawn and asphalt between them.

"You followed me to my house?" Aimee asks sharply.

The fat girl says nothing, does nothing. Waits.

"What are you *doing* here?" Aimee asks, meaner this time.

Nothing. The fat girl is a boulder.

"You know, I don't know if you think I can't see you when you're, like, following me around all the time, but I totally can, I see you watching me, and it's really wicked creepy." Aimee sticks her chin out—*that's right, I said "creepy"*—but at the same time pulls the box of her folded arms into her chest—for what, for protection? What does she think the fat girl is gonna do, blow?

The fat girl shifts her weight from one great leg to the other, making a kind of rippling wave move through her body. Aimee thinks this is a sign that she's about to say something, but a few seconds pass and she's still standing there, silent. Aimee takes a forceful step forward and it's like she pressed a trigger somewhere:

"Careful," the fat girl says. Aimee halts. The voice that comes out of the fat girl is a murmur, a hum, almost like the sound of a dishwasher or dryer. For a second Aimee's not even sure that she's spoken.

"What did you say?" Aimee asks warily.

The fat girl takes a wheezy breath.

"Be careful with Cara." It's like her voice isn't even exactly coming from her mouth; it's like it's coming from all around her, like she's amplified through a hidden microphone or something.

"Cara Roy?"

The fat girl nods the smallest nod, barely perceptible to the naked eye.

"Why?" Aimee can't help herself. "What's wrong with Cara?"

The fat girl shrugs, a tiny shift of her shoulders.

"Why are you telling me this? Why are you following me around all the time? How did you find out where I live?" Aimee feels a little coil of hysteria start to rise in her gut. The buzz starts back up in her ears—the threat, the promise, of losing control.

"I just wanted to warn you," the fat girl says, lips barely moving.

"About Cara. You think you can trust her, but you can't."

As if she's feeling bolder now, the fat girl brings a swollen hand up to brush her bangs aside, revealing her eyes, which have softened into normal, blinking gray eyes—human eyes.

"I know how she can make you feel."

"Uh, you don't know how she makes me feel," Aimee says, but it comes out sounding insecure, more a timid question than a forceful objection. Then she regains her confidence in a sudden bright burst. "Look, I don't know what your deal is with Cara, but me and her being friends is none of your business. And I don't know who told you you could follow people around and like, *spy* on them, like like *stalk* them, but it's extremely not okay and if you don't stop I'm gonna report you. I mean to the cops, okay? I'm not kidding."

The fat girl doesn't react.

Louder, Aimee says, "I'll call them right now if you don't stop trespassing on my property. I'll go inside and call them right now."

The fat girl's stillness only deepens.

Aimee feels the fat girl's motionlessness, her immense, powerful nothingness, spreading like new gravity over her own body, falling over her brain in a thin gray mist, slowing her heartbeat, lowering her blood pressure—entrancing her entire being. It seems to Aimee, without looking down at herself, that her edges are starting to blur. It's as if she can feel the world around her melting into and through her newly transparent hands and arms and feet. The fat girl's stillness fogs Aimee's consciousness like a sweet-smelling noxious gas.

Aimee shakes her head once to clear it, then finds her voice again, strong.

"If this is your idea of trying to make friends with someone,"

Aimee says, clear and biting as a winter morning, "then you are sick. You are, you're sick and disgusting. Leave me alone from now on, okay? Don't even look in my direction. I don't ever want to catch you spying on me again."

There's a second's pause while Aimee waits, eyes locked on the fat girl's face. Then the fat girl drops her eyelids like window shades. She gives her hair a minute shake—no more than a shiver—and the hair she had moved aside slips back over her face. Sealed up again behind eyes and bangs, she turns to go—pivots in place and backs up slightly, like a car pulling out of a parking space. Then drifts off heavily down the driveway.

Aimee stands watching her go, trembling in her knees and elbows and wrists.

Inside, still shaking, Aimee drops her bag on the kitchen floor and dials Bill's number. He picks up with a clatter and a muffled swear, then:

"Poetry hotline, what's the nature of your poetic emergency?"

Bill's voice is warm and sweaty; Aimee recognizes it immediately as his three-beer voice. In the background there's a burst of laughter, the sound of a group of people loosened up and ready to roar.

"Hello caller?" Bill brays again. "Please state the nature and location of your emergency so that our trained poetry technicians may assist you."

"Bill, it's me."

"Oh heyyy!" Bill's voice slides down into an oilier register. "Baby, where are you? Get over here, the party's started."

It takes a second before Aimee can say, "Bill, it's *Aimee*."

And another second goes by before Bill clears his throat and says, "Aimee. Uh, hi."

"Can I talk to you for a second?" Aimee shields the mouthpiece of the phone with her hand and glances furtively out the breakfast-nook window, like a victim of domestic violence in a Lifetime movie trying to orchestrate her secret escape.

"Ame, you know I love to talk to you but this isn't the greatest time." The crowd noise behind Bill fades, as if he's taken the phone into another room.

"I know, I can tell you're having a party, but can I just quickly tell you about—"

"It's not a party, it's not actually a party," Bill interrupts hastily. "It's a meeting. It's all English Department people here and we're just, we're working on the spring course list. And hey, Ame, I'm sorry about what I said just now. I thought you were somebody else for a second."

"Whatever, that's cool."

"I wouldn't say something"—Bill clears his throat again awkwardly—"inappropriate like that to you on purpose."

"Yeah, it's really okay." At this moment Aimee truly couldn't care less whether Bill has skeezy girls coming over to his apartment or not. She's desperate to talk to him about the fat girl.

"Actually," Bill goes on, "what it is, is that Marcus is here, you remember my friend Marcus? And his girlfriend is supposed to come and she's late and I thought you were her. That's all it is."

"Whatever, Bill, it's really totally cool. Can I just ask you about something really quickly?"

"Just . . . *really* quickly," Bill says. "Then I gotta get back to this meeting."

"Okay, remember I told you about the fat girl?" Aimee talks fast.

"Uh . . ."

"Remember on the first day of school, remember I saw that fat girl getting chased down the hall and you said write about her?"

"Yeah, okay."

"It doesn't even matter if you remember, there's this fat girl and she's been following me around and kind of spying on me all the time and today she showed up at our house. At our house, Bill! Just now!"

"At Riverglade?"

"Yes! She was waiting for me when I got home! I don't know how she found out where I live but she was waiting for me in the driveway when I got off the bus and she was acting really freaky and she tried to tell me not to be friends with this one girl and I don't even know why she *cares* who I'm friends with because I don't even know her, I've never hardly even talked to her, and I feel like she's watching me all the time everywhere I go and what should I do, Bill? Should I call the police?"

"Are you scared she's going to hurt you? Is she dangerous, this fat girl?" Bill seems to be sobering up a little.

"Well, I don't know. Maybe a little. Not really."

"Is she like, armed?"

"Um, no. I don't think she's armed."

"Okay, so I think, rule of thumb: unless somebody's armed and dangerous you don't need to call the police on them. Generally."

"Okay but what if she comes back? Bill, what do I do if she comes back again?"

"Well have you tried talking to her?"

"I told her she was trespassing and to get off my property or I'd call the cops."

"Okay, so you threatened her, but did you *talk* to her? Did you try to get to know her?"

"Like *how*? *How* am I supposed to get to know her, what am I supposed to do, be like, 'Excuse me, hi, I noticed you're constantly following me around like a psycho, would you like to hang out and share your deepest feelings with me?' Is that what you're suggesting?"

Aimee can practically hear Bill rolling his eyes.

"Does that sound like something I would suggest?"

"Well then what are you telling me I should say?"

"It's easy, just say—"

A long, feminine peal of laughter ribbons through the background on Bill's end. Then a muffled squelching sound, as if Bill has put his palm over the receiver. The *murph-murph-murph* of a conversation whose words Aimee can't make out. Then Bill comes back on, clear.

"Okay, so right, so try that."

"Try what? Try *what*? You were about to tell me what to say and then someone laughed and you cut yourself off! What should I say to her, Bill? What should I say?" Aimee feels panic rising in her chest.

"Okay, first of all, you need to chill. Can you chill for a second? And breathe with me?"

Aimee nods in her empty kitchen.

"I don't hear you breathing."

Aimee inhales a lungful of air and exhales it noisily, extra loud so Bill can hear.

"Okay, better. Are you slightly less hysterical now?"

"Uh-hunh," says Aimee tightly.

"Because if you're hysterical you're not going to listen to a word I'm saying."

"I'm listening, Bill, I'm listening, I'm listening."

"What you say to her is, you ask her what she wants. You say, 'Hey, sister, how come you're following me around all the time?'"

"'Hey, sister'?" Aimee echoes, dismayed.

"Or whatever lingo you kids prefer these days. 'Hey, man,' you say, 'what gives with this behavior? What is it you want from me, and how can I give it to you so you can stop following me around all the time?' How's that?"

Slowly Aimee sinks down until she's sitting on the kitchen floor. She leans her head back against the wall beneath the phone.

"Bill," she says sadly, "that totally sucks. I would never in a million years say that to this girl."

"Well then Ame, I'm cashed. That's my best advice. If she's not two seconds away from hacking you up with a machete and you're too afraid to talk to her like a human being then I guess you're just going to have to get used to having a stalker. It's actually kind of cool, if you think about it. She probably just senses your brilliance and wants to be near you just to soak it up."

"Shut up," says Aimee glumly. "No way."

"Way," Bill drawls, amusing himself now. "I bet that's it, Ame. She can tell you're going to be a famous poet someday, and she wants to get a piece of you before you get huge. Hey, what if you got so famous you were the first poet ever to be chased by the paparazzi?"

"Bill, come on."

"What if you were the first poet ever to have your picture in *Us Weekly*? 'Poets—They're Just Like Us!'"

"Bill, will you please be serious for a second?"

"Bill, do we have any Corona or is there just the Dos Equis in the cooler?"

Female voice. Perfectly nice voice. Perfectly nice boring female voice. Aimee feels her heart and stomach get up and shuffle around, trying clumsily to switch places inside her.

"Aimee," Bill says, apologetic, "I gotta go. Someone's . . . I gotta get back to this meeting."

"Yeah," says Aimee, "uh-hunh."

She beeps off the phone as fast as she can, before she can hear Bill hang up on her.

• 11 •

Meghan's mind is a blank. Meghan's vision is a tunnel. Meghan's body moves like an animal's body through the woods behind Riverglade Estates, following the shortcut she knows by heart along the banks of the trickly Thorn Creek, crashing through the tree branches that hang over the path, stumbling through the pricker bushes that reach out to embrace her, ripping away from them as they cling to her, trying to suck her in. She feels nothing, sees nothing. The sound of nothing is a roar in her ears.

Not far now to the place she goes to immerse herself completely in nothing.

She bursts out of the woods and there it is, her sanctuary, the dying barn, floating like a garbage barge in the middle of the cornfield. Meghan makes a lumbering beeline for it, crunching through the yellow knee-high cornstalks. At last she's there, turns sideways to get through the hole in the wall—three boards missing make a door—and inside it's cool and dark, dappled with stripes of dusty sunshine slanting through the open slats in the walls. So filthy and so familiar—the sag of the roof in the middle of the space, the shadowy shapes of debris: heaps of rotting timber, piles of tin cans, the old tractor rusting into sculpture in the corner. Dirt floor overgrown with weeds and grass.

Meghan makes for her spot by the wall, unshoulders her backpack and lets it drop to the ground, sits down with a dusty thud on the scratchy horse blanket she brought here years ago. Breathes in the smell of earth and decay, so thick it's like the taste of a stew in her mouth. Wills the heaving drumbeat of her heart to slow. Breathes in, out. In, out.

Like dragons the memories fly up from the dark pit inside her— she tries to bat them away but they circle her, flapping their leathery wings—

Meghan and Cara, eight years old, fifty feet up in the hemlock tree, giggling—Meghan and Cara, nine years old, pressed against each other on the Tilt-A-Whirl at the town fair, screaming—Meghan's ten-year-old hands French braiding Cara's red hair—eleven-year-old Cara grinning through her headgear at Meghan like a puffy-mouthed boxer—

Feverishly Meghan gropes for her backpack and unzips the front pocket where she keeps her emergency supplies. She plunges her hand in and grabs the first thing she finds, tears open the Snickers bar and bites off more than half of it—its saturated sweetness blooms in her mouth, but it's not nearly enough—

Cara's bedroom, pistachio-ice-cream green with the stenciled pattern of acorns and squirrels around the ceiling—Cara's seashell collection, Cara's jewelry box, Cara's sparkling collection of pierced earrings, the charm bracelet with the hearts and stars Cara's grandmother gave her—the smell of Cara's mother's kitchen, a mixture of milk and onions—the smell of lilacs drifting onto Cara's screened-in porch during sleepovers in the spring—

The second half of the Snickers bar is still coming apart in her mouth, and Meghan's arm is already elbow-deep in the backpack, rummaging around for reinforcements—

The reading group that Mrs. Jackson made up just for them, because they were the two best readers in fourth grade, so that they got to read chapter books and make dioramas while everyone else was still filling out dumb reading comp sheets about The Life of Amelia Earhart or whatever—the feeling Meghan got every day when it was time for Language Arts and she got to go off with Cara to work in the corner, like they were the only two members of their own special club, and everyone else knew they belonged to each other—the feeling Meghan had that no matter how chubby she was, no matter how gross, no matter how many times other kids asked her when the baby was due or how much her farts weighed, Cara would always make her feel safe, Cara would never leave her place by Meghan's side—

Butterfinger bar melting on her tongue, gumming up the crevices in her teeth; the salty sweetness floods her mind like a wave breaking on a beach, but then ebbs, slipping back into the sea, and the memories only come on faster and stronger—

Summer after sixth grade, when Meghan started ferrying messages between Cara and Jamie Bartlett. . . . Skinny, sandy-haired Jamie Bartlett, who lived two streets down from Meghan and Cara on Vernon Road, with his friendly fluffy white dog named Gwendolyn and his friendly parents named Mike and Elaine and his friendly big sister named Marcie, who once gave Meghan a free box of Girl Scout cookies for no reason. . . . Jamie Bartlett, who shot hoops in his driveway every day from five to six P.M., where Meghan would reliably find him when she emerged from the bushes clutching a message from Cara. . . . Jamie Bartlett, who smiled at her and biffed her shoulder like a buddy and called her "Megster," as in, "Hiya Megster, whatcha have for me today?" What she had for him today was a little love note, on pink-inked graph paper that Cara had spritzed with her mother's Shalimar perfume. Two or three times a week Meghan brought them, little love notes written in pink glitter pen, folded into tight little triangles or squares. Little love notes that told Jamie where to meet Cara (in the old toolshed behind the abandoned house on Sunset Avenue, usually) the next afternoon that Cara didn't have cello or ballet—

Hostess Cupcakes, two thick gulps, dark sweet empty taste—
Hostess Twinkies, two soft gulps, light sweet empty taste—

The empty feeling that crept through Meghan on those afternoons when Cara didn't have cello or ballet, when Cara and Jamie holed up together inside the windowless, falling-down shed and Meghan was in charge of watching out for intruders—kids or grown-ups, anyone who might invade their privacy. The way time stretched out while Meghan sat there on the rotting tree stump ten feet away, shoulders slumped, watching the shadows inch across the grass, half wanting to sneak over and press her ear to the shed door, half afraid of what she might hear if she did. And the long, hollow feeling she would get after they emerged (always Cara first—Meghan would see Jamie slip out a second later and disappear off in the other direction), Cara dreamy and happy, not really paying attention to Meghan, not really talking to her all the way home. But still, it was not until seventh grade started—

And she is eating with both hands now, supply pocket starting to empty out—panicky feeling fluttering in her chest: *What if there's not enough?* Smartfood, salty cheesy handfuls, Reese's Pieces, crunchy melty mouthfuls, and at last Meghan starts to feel the stirrings of anesthesia tingling at the ends of her fingers and toes. Still—

First day of seventh grade, speechless with terror and fatter than she'd ever been before, Meghan walked into her new homeroom to see Jamie Bartlett, taller than he had been before he went to basketball camp, blonder than he had been before he went to basketball camp, surrounded by a bunch of other guys all wearing the same maroon basketball camp T-shirt he was wearing. They were sitting on top of their desks, forming a solid mass of boy, a block of shoulders and shorts in the corner. Jamie Bartlett looked up at Meghan as she came through the door and made an icy band of eye contact with her, and a threat passed from his eyes to hers, like a fish darting through a pass in the rocks: *You don't speak to me. You don't look at me. You make like you don't even know me anymore. And if you ever tell anyone what went on in that shed . . .* Meghan could feel the silent dot dot dot, the promise of punishments too dark to describe. She blinked at him, dropped her eyes to the floor, and went silently to the other side of the room to sit down. And when Ms. Rosenberg took attendance that first morning of seventh grade and said, "Bartlett, James? Is James Bartlett here?" blonder, taller Jamie Bartlett raised his hand and said, "Yo. Call me J-Bar."

Quick, then, the rest of it, quick and total—in a matter of weeks her whole life collapsed. Seventh-grade Cara, still trying at first to get Jamie Bartlett to be her boyfriend, not seeing, as Meghan saw, that there *was* no more Jamie Bartlett, there was only J-Bar, JV Basketball King, who was not about to have a dorky teacher's pet like Cara for a girlfriend. Seventh-grade Cara, one September afternoon on the bus, looking at Meghan sitting beside her with a cold new disgust, as if she'd been blindfolded all the years of their friendship and only now saw the monster that Meghan really was. Only now saw how Meghan was holding her back. Seventh-grade Cara explaining to Meghan calmly that she wouldn't be able to hang out with Meghan during school anymore because she was trying to change her image a little, no offense. Then seventh-grade Cara pretending she wasn't home when Meghan called; seventh-grade Cara pretending she had too much math homework to do to come over. And finally, by October of seventh grade, Cara Roy turning Meghan Ball into the Amazing Vanishing Girl, gazing right through her when Meghan passed her in the halls, as if Meghan had become a ghost, a vapor.

And then, adrift, abandoned in the halls of the junior high, with no one to watch her back or come to her rescue . . . J-Bar and his crew circling her for the first time in the hallway outside homeroom, the pack of them closing in . . . the falling sensation of becoming prey . . . the words they said to her lost now in memory but their smiling faces unforgettable . . . the blank look on Cara's face as she passed behind them and caught Meghan's eye for the fleetingest instant . . .

Meghan's memory catches like a glitch on a CD, plays the same moment over and over again:

Meghan's mouth opening. Her voice tiny and useless, saying, "Cara." Saying, "Cara." Cara seeing her. Cara turning. Cara vanishing in the crowd. The boys pressing in on all sides. Their teeth and claws sinking into her flesh. Then a blank spot, a white flash, over the memory of being devoured.

Meghan pauses for a second in the barn to catch her breath, which is trapped in little bubbles in between wet wads of Cheetos in her mouth and throat. In, out. In, out. Chewing with her mouth open, wheezing as she chews. The tingling has spread up her arms and legs now—a buzzing blankness, like a staticky TV channel. Soon it will swirl up through her gut, slip up over her heart and lungs like lukewarm water, flood through her throat and mouth and head—drown her in nothingness. Meghan slows down—she can coast to the end now. She takes the last Hershey bar from the backpack half reluctantly, slips a fingertip under its silver flap, wanting both to gobble it down and hurl it away at the same time.

The fat girl who loses her only friend sees, all at once, how everything works. She sees that all promises are fictions, all friendships are games with winners and losers. The fat girl left alone in the world sees that every human being has a value assigned to them that they are helpless to change no matter what they do, and she sees that people trade each other like baseball cards: three cheap friends for two valuable friends, a whole group of worthless friends for one popular friend. It's like dying and coming back to life, being a fat girl who loses her only friend; it gives you an insight into the people around you that the average person couldn't bear to have.

But if it doesn't break her, this insight makes the friendless fat girl strong. The fat girl left alone in the world becomes the ultimate outsider, and outsiders always know the insiders' secrets, because insiders don't care what's happening on the outside—they never check to see what the outsiders know. They usually don't even know who the outsiders are. The person on the bottom sees what's happening on top, the person at the back sees what's happening in front, the person on the outside sees what's happening at the center, and the fat girl who loses her only friend is under, behind, and outside all at once; if she cares to look, she can see everything in every direction. God must be a friendless fat girl, because only friendless fat girls are as omniscient as God.

The final collapse into oblivion that accompanies the last mouthful. Bursting—the pressure of her gut against the waistband of her pants the only feeling left in her body. Meghan undoes the button of her fly and unzips it, spreads out, feeling the rapture of the deep lapping at her from all sides. Surrounded by the wreckage of the binge, eviscerated wrappers like the husks of dead insects all around her, Meghan leans her head back against the barn wall and blacks out.

• 12 •

"It gives me great pleasure to announce to you the winner of this year's Autumn Poetry Competition, sponsored by *Photon*"—Mr. Handsley pauses a moment to build anticipation—"Miss Cara Roy!"

The temporary classroom bursts into frenzied applause. Moira Dahlquist clasps her hands together and presses them to her heart like she's Cara's proud mother. At first Cara looks startled, then transforms into Cinderella at the ball, lips parted—me? *really?*—looking down bashfully, shaking her head in amazement.

Aimee feels a little twig of disappointment snap in her chest, quick and light, at the moment when Mr. Handsley says Cara's name. But then she looks over at Cara, blushing and shrugging, and feels a genuine rush of happiness for her. Cara works harder than anyone Aimee has ever met, and she's been the nicest person in the entire school to Aimee. How can Aimee be even a little jealous when Cara has been nothing but generous to her, nothing but encouraging, nothing but incredibly sweet and supportive? Cara deserves to win.

"In singling out Miss Roy's work for distinction, the judges commented on its, quote, inventiveness of structure, provocative line breaks, sophisticated use of punctuation, and arresting imagery, unquote." Cara blushes furiously. Becky Trainer can barely contain herself, claps her hands in front of her chest like a bird fluttering its wings, a little trilly clap. Mr. Handsley continues: "As you all know, the winning poem will be read during morning announcements on Monday, in place of the usual published poem slaughtered—excuse me, read—by the redoubtable Ms. Champoux." The girls titter nervously and Cara rolls her eyes. "Then the poem will be sent on to Washington, D.C., to be evaluated by a distinguished panel of judges. Ms. Roy, will you do us the favor of reading aloud your winning poem now? A special preview, just for your co-editors?"

Cara starts to make a fuss about not wanting to take valuable time away from the group.

"C'mon," urges Moira.

"Please?" begs Becky.

"We want to hear it!" bawls Yael.

With a show of reluctance Cara gets to her feet and takes the paper with her poem on it from Mr. Handsley. Right before she begins to read, as she opens her mouth to inhale for the first word, Cara shoots a look at Aimee, her eyes alive with the sparkle of intimacy, an only-you-can-really-understand-this look, an it's-just-you-and-me-against-the-world look. Cara's look enters Aimee and warms her whole body. Deep in her cold chest, Aimee's heart light glows.

"'Hunger Strike,'" pronounces Cara, "by Cara Roy."

The room falls into respectful silence.

> *"I am carved like David,*
> *every line of my body perfectly chiseled.*
> *Hunger is the blade that has made me smooth.*
> *I am a statue, yet I am only air at my center.*
> *I go to hug myself and*
> *—poof!—*
> *my arms go right through me*
> *finding nothing to hold on to.*
> *My hands meet behind my own back*
> *in a stone handshake.*
> *This is not what you were expecting.*
> *I'm so cold.*
> *I'm so sharp.*
> *I've been cut, now I'll cut you.*
> *Come closer.*
> *Yes, come closer to me.*
> *I am going to make you see what I see."*

A moment in which the world tilts to the left, warps, and constricts. Aimee feels herself pressed into its angle, suddenly deaf, all the breath squeezed out of her—stunned.

Somewhere in the distance: a burst of applause.

Cara, far away although she's right across the room, looks up from her paper directly at Aimee, *directly* at her, and smiles the exact same warm, humble smile she gave her before she started to read, exactly the same as every other smile she's ever given her. Just as if she hasn't just ripped off Aimee's deepest, most private thoughts and passed them off as her own.

It's not *exactly* the same poem. It's not word for word. But it's Aimee's poem. It's the poem she worked over excruciatingly closely, the only one she ever revised the way Bill told her to. It's got her poem's heartbeat, her poem's fingerprints, at least two-thirds of her poem's DNA. It's even wearing her poem's shoes—that last line!

Aimee starts trembling. The temporary classroom is chiming with adulation, girls exclaiming to Cara, to each other, how brilliant she is, how brave. From across the room Aimee sees Mr. Handsley eyeing her curiously, arms folded across his chest, head tipped to one side. That's when she notices that she's the only one not clapping, the only one silent in a room full of cheer. She knows she has to join in or people will know something is up, but her hands are dead on the desk in front of her, she can't make them move. And all along the column of her spine she can feel coming like a train speeding toward her, gathering speed and sound and intensity, a reaction like none she has ever had before. With nothing in her mouth to bring it on. The sizzle rises to a roar in her ears and she knows that in less than thirty seconds all five of her senses will be consumed in a silver fire. She has to get out of there before they all see it.

Aimee gets to her feet and bolts from the room.

The girls' room smells like old pee and paper towels—Aimee makes it into the last stall and pulls the door shut behind her before the howling metallic waves crash over her. The floor billows up around her like a gray-tiled sail—the cinder-block walls ripple in and press against her on all sides. The reaction is inside her and outside her at the same time, a pulsing, glittering helix of noise and tremor.

Nothing, Aimee keeps hearing at the back of her mind, in the one tiny space that hasn't been completely engulfed by the reaction. *I've eaten nothing all day, nothing, nothing, nothing.*

This must be how the body reacts to deception. This must be how the immune system fights off the feeling of being violated by a friend. This must be what it's like to have every white blood cell in your system come rushing to attack a morsel of betrayal on your tongue.

It's hours before Aimee stumbles out the front door of the school and scans the parking lot for the presidential Jeep. She spots it, with Cara standing beside it, over by the access road leading to the playing fields. Aimee weaves her way through the parked cars and calls out, as soon as she gets within shouting range, "Cara. Hey, Cara!"

Cara turns around and blossoms into openmouthed joy when she sees Aimee coming.

"Hey, you, where did you get to in there? We missed you during the rest of the meeting!"

"Yeah, I had something to—I had a, um, thing." Aimee swallows. How is she going to get these words out of her mouth without breaking them into bits?

"What is it?" Cara's face morphs into a portrait of concern. "What's wrong, Aimee, is something wrong?"

"Your poem—" Aimee begins.

As if she's flipped an invisible switch, Cara's face changes back instantly to sweet, glowing pleasure. "Thank you so much," she says before Aimee has a chance to finish. "I knew that poem would speak to you. I really wrote it with you in mind."

"With my *poem* in mind," Aimee blurts out.

Cara's face empties of expression for a split second, goes as blank as the screen of a dead TV set. Then her brow knits into the shape of confusion.

"What do you mean?"

"You *know* what I mean."

"No, I don't."

She's going to make me actually say it. Aimee relaxes her mouth, tries to loosen her tongue.

"You . . . you . . . copied my poem," Aimee breathes.

Cara raises her eyebrows in shock. "What are you *talking* about?"

"You, I—your poem is, basically a total copy of mine, the one I read to you and gave you to keep at your house." Aimee can't tell if she's about to faint or throw up or burst into tears.

Cara shakes her head slowly side to side in stunned disbelief.

"What are you *saying*?" she asks tremulously, her eyes shining with the beginnings of tears. "You're accusing me of . . . Aimee, I . . . God, I don't even know what to say." Cara fights to maintain her composure, breathing heavily and swallowing hard.

"Say you'll take it back," Aimee says quietly. "Go back in there and tell Mr. Handsley you want to withdraw your poem from the competition."

Now Cara stares at Aimee stonily.

"I just won the competition. You want me to go in there and tell our advisor that I withdraw my poem from the competition, after I just won? Because why, am I supposed to tell him? Because I didn't actually write it? Is that what you want me to say to him?"

"Well, um, you didn't."

A flicker of anger darkens Cara's clear eyes.

"I—I mean, I hardly know what to say to you right now, because I can't believe you would walk up to me and talk to me like this, like we don't even have—like we never even had—I mean, okay, I'm not going to deny that there are some common themes in our two poems, but that's only because of what we were talking about when you came over! Maybe you don't remember that we had a whole conversation about how I had the same experiences as the ones you were writing about? And we talked all about how your poem reminded me of that terrible, awful time in my life and like, took me right back to when I used to be sick? And I'm sorry but I actually thought that conversation was *meaningful*, I thought we were like, *connecting* at that moment, and like *sharing* something, and getting *close*. And now you're accusing me of . . . plagiarizing your ideas?"

Cara has worked herself up into a tearful rage; her face is burning pink and her hairline is damp with sweat.

"I . . ." In the face of Cara's wild, torn-up anger Aimee feels the resolve to expose her faltering.

"I guess it's sort of amazing to me that you weren't feeling that at all. I guess I sort of feel like an idiot. Here I thought we were bonding in a serious way at that moment and becoming the kind of friends who could share really deep, really scary things with each other, and you were, what? Faking it the whole time? I mean, I never told anyone before about how I used to be sick. I never told anyone about Carol. You're the first person I ever talked to about that stuff, and I would never have admitted any of it to you and told you all my secrets like that if I thought you were going to make me pay for it like this. I guess I was just totally wrong about you."

Now Cara cries for real, covering her face with her hands.

Aimee's at a loss for words. On the one hand she wants to put her arms around Cara and comfort her, say No no no, I'm sorry, take me back, trust me again, we *were* bonding! Be my best friend and don't ever leave my side! But something keeps her from begging like that—a scrap of steel lodged in her heart that says, No no no, stand up for yourself.

"I'm sorry?" she ventures noncommittally.

"Whatever." Cara turns away to unlock the Jeep door, then pivots back around to face Aimee, her eyes hard. "I just think you need to remember," she says, "that nobody owns ideas. Ideas belong to everybody. You think you've had some special unique experience that only you can describe but actually a million other people have had that same experience, and they might describe it just the way that you would. And um, that's why poetry *works*, by the way. If we were all totally unique and special we wouldn't ever understand each other when we talked or wrote. The only reason we can love another person's poems is because we're all basically the same, we know what other people are talking about because we've had the same experiences they have. You might have been hungry but so have I. You don't own hungry. Remember that, Aimee."

Wordlessly Aimee watches as Cara slips into the driver's seat of the Jeep, pulls the door shut, and drives away.

At home Aimee dials Bill's number and sits down numbly at the kitchen table, waiting to hear his voice. But Bill's phone just rings, and rings, and rings.

There is no Aimee Zorn.

Fog morning, dull morning. Smoke and mist.

Meghan searches for no one in the crowd outside school.

Inside the front hall Meghan scans for no particular hat, no particular skirt, no particular boots. Kids swirl around her, undifferentiated as surf. Words fall from mouths in shattered fragments:

"—totally and I was like what and she—"

"—gave me one that freaking sucks can you—"

"—didn't you told you to—"

"—shut it—"

"—him stupid—"

"—yeah but homework whatever—"

"—I said anyway—"

"—anyway—"

Words break like waves on the rock of Meghan's ear. The meaninglessness makes Meghan long for silence.

The first bell rings.

Meghan looks around for no one, makes a note of nothing, and heads for homeroom.

There is no Aimee Zorn.

"Good morning students faculty and staff it is. My pleasure to welcome you. To Thursday. Morning."

No J-Bar this morning in homeroom. Nothing to worry about or keep tabs on in her peripheral vision. Still Meghan's head aches dully, a vine of pain growing around and through it.

"This morning we have for. Morning meditation. Eh selection from thee poet Langford Hayes thee poet Langley Hoyes thee *ahem. Ahem.* Poet Lang . . . ston Hughes."

Kids are paying attention to nothing, staring out the windows and up at the ceiling; the heat is on and it's stuffy and the whole room feels stupid. Meghan's eyes are shrinking in their sockets.

"Please listen and remain. Listening for thirty seconds after thee. Selection concludes."

Meghan's whole self is draining into a hole at her center. Her edges collapse in as she slowly implodes.

"'A Dream Deferred,'" drones Ms. Champoux.

Going to class is not going to work today; Meghan makes an executive decision to go AWOL.

Mr. Cox is lodged at his desk, shoulders hunched like a gargoyle, glowering down at the morning memo and waiting for the poem to be over.

Meghan doesn't even make the effort to disappear. She just gets up, slings her backpack over one shoulder, and walks quietly up to the front of the room. If anyone notices her go, no one has the energy to say anything about it. She's alone and moving through the empty sophomore hall in seconds.

There is no Aimee Zorn.

Music Practice Room D opens to anyone's touch now; somebody—nobody—busted the trick lock so that it stays open all the time. It's only a matter of time before the stoner kids or gaming kids discover this fact and colonize the room for themselves. Meghan steps in and surveys the damage. Somebody—nobody—has left three curled foil Jell-O cup covers on top of the piano. Sticky garbage. Somebody—nobody—has no respect for this space.

Meghan closes her eyes and turns 360 degrees, slowly and deliberately, trying to vanish, but she can feel the persistent presence of someone—no one!—who never should have been in this room in the first place. It feels like there's static in the corners of the room, cobwebs of dirty energy. Meghan turns and turns, trying to clear the air, trying to make the room magic—and *hers*—again. Sixteen times around and she's getting dizzy, and she hasn't even started to disappear. No one has ruined the only safe space Meghan ever had in this school.

There is no Aimee Zorn.

Late in the day. Meghan floats, exhausted, in the dark of the sick room, tethered lightly to the vinyl bed but hovering a couple of inches above the wax paper surface, buoyed by currents of warm, rising air. Mrs. Chuddy's words spill over her ears, her skin, her closed eyes, falling into coherence and then scattering into sparkles like the reflection of sun on rippling water.

"... heard them going at it all, yes, afternoon ... deeper but what he didn't say then ... oh yes skating he's skating on very thin ice ... never would have if I didn't ... no no ... so worried about him ... three strikes he's gone ... Deborah and Myra said ... yes I said ... said ..."

Meghan phases in and out of twilight sleep, floats and dozes and bobs.

Nobody comes in with an allergic reaction. Nobody lies down on the bed beside her. Nobody curls away from her on the crinkly wax paper, and Meghan lies in the dark not waiting for no one.

• 14 •

Aimee wakes to the sensation that her left eyelid is being pried open by a crowbar of sunlight.

She rolls over and her bones clank against the floor she's lying on like old tools rattling against the bottom of a junk drawer. She peels both sticky eyes open and finds herself on the floor of Bill's study, in a tangle of blankets taken off her own bed. The sun is pouring through the unshaded windows, lighting the room as loudly as the blast from a foghorn. Dimly, like a scene from a movie she saw long ago, Aimee remembers stumbling in here late last night after lying awake in her own bed for hours, too scrambled with stuttery thoughts of Cara to fall asleep. Bill's brown shag carpet must have cast a spell over her as powerful as the Wicked Witch of the West's field of poppies—she doesn't even remember lying down on it before she passed out.

From the other end of the hall come the sounds of her mother going through her morning bathroom routine—the shush and silence of water being turned on and off, the clatter of a dropped lip-stick hitting the sink. If her mother's already doing her makeup it's late—she'll be heading out to the Toyota soon, and suddenly Aimee knows that if she is discovered here, having slept on Bill's floor, it will somehow constitute a serious betrayal. It will somehow be a very big deal, and she will somehow be in very big trouble. Hurriedly she gets up, tugging the blanket nest around her shoulders like a huge heavy stole, and eases the door to Bill's office open.

The coast is clear, and Aimee scuttles back to her bedroom. She heaves herself, covers and all, across her bed, so that her head is hanging off one side and her feet are hanging off the other. As soon as she hits the mattress she hears the click of the bathroom door opening, and moments later her mother is standing beside her. Aimee's head is so close to the floor that all she can see are her mother's nylon-shimmery shins and navy blue Naturalizers, but she can feel the air change shape above her as her mother puts her hands on her hips.

"Honey, you're sick?" her mom asks, both weary and concerned.

Aimee nods her hanging head.

"Come up here and let me look at you." Her mother settles on the edge of Aimee's bed and Aimee hoists herself up with a groaning show of exhaustion, as if she's extracting her head from a bog where it's been buried for centuries. She rubs her eyes with the backs of her hands, uncrusting their corners, and peers out blearily at her mom.

Her mother is morning-perfect, dry where she should be dry and glossy wet where she should be glossy wet. Her just-styled hair is both a solid and a liquid, a blonde breeze frozen mid-swirl around her head. Her silk-blend blouse flows into two neat collar points on either side of her neck; at her waist it's tucked in crisply, like a beautifully wrapped present.

She puts her cool hand on Aimee's forehead and peers at it, as if trying to read words developing in magic ink on her own skin.

"You don't have a fever, but you're clammy. Actually your temperature feels a little low. And look at these circles under your eyes—did you sleep at all last night?"

Aimee shrugs noncommittally.

Her mother swallows, preparing herself for something.

"Can I ask what you ate yesterday?"

Aimee looks away.

"Honey . . ." Aimee's mother takes her palm off Aimee's forehead and folds her hands tensely in her lap. "I know you might not feel up to it right now, but we have to have a Conversation."

Aimee groans and collapses back against her nest of blankets. "Now?" she objects.

"Yes, honey, now. This Conversation is really long overdue."

"Don't you have to get to work?"

"*I'll* pay attention to when I have to get to work. *You* pay attention to the question I asked you. What did you eat yesterday?"

"I was getting sick!" Aimee cries.

Her mother shakes her head grimly, and Aimee sees that her hands are trembling as she smoothes her tweedy skirt out over her thighs.

"Sweetheart, I think it's safe to say that part of the reason you're sick right now is because you're not eating a balanced diet anymore.

Food is fuel, you know. Food is what keeps our bodies healthy and strong."

Aimee rolls her eyes. Is this going to be a Conversation about basic health facts?

"Honey, listen, I've been reading about this and—"

"Reading about *what*?" Aimee demands.

"About . . ." Her mother adjusts the hem of her skirt. "About different eating problems that people sometimes have, and—"

"I don't *have* an eating problem," Aimee asserts. "I have allergies to a couple of foods, that's all."

"I know, I know that's how it feels to you. And you know that I'm committed to giving you your space and not trying to control your decisions. You know that when I was growing up my mother imposed a lot of things on me about the kind of person she wanted me to be, and I have tried very hard not to do that with you. I have tried as much as possible to respect you as an individual and let you take responsibility for yourself. But honey, this is getting out of hand. Even you have to admit that it's getting out of hand. Whole days go by now where I never see you eat, I don't know whether you ever eat at school, and now you're starting to get sick—"

"I eat every, single, day," Aimee declares, hitting each word hard and clear, like a xylophone bar.

"Okay." Her mother looks sad. "I believe you if you say that you do. But all the same, I think it's time for a visit to Dr. Petrarca."

"No!" Aimee sits bolt upright out of her nest of blankets.

"Honey, we need some professional help. Even if it's just allergies, you never used to have allergies like this, so if you've developed them all of a sudden, something could be seriously wrong."

"Mom, I'm fine. I'm handling it and I'm fine!"

The thought of visiting Dr. Petrarca, the big-bellied, fake-jolly, rubber-smelling pediatrician, makes Aimee weak with dread.

"This isn't going to be a big deal. We'll just ask him to recommend an allergy specialist for us to talk to"—her mother swallows, then blurts out the next part all in a rush—"and maybe he knows a good psychologist and maybe he'll know about some nutritional supplements we can give you to help keep you nourished while you're staying away from the foods that make you feel bad."

Psychologist. Nutritional supplements. Revulsion surges into Aimee's throat as she flashes back on Cara's description of the protein shakes—she imagines a tube of thick white liquid spiraling toward her, tasteless as tile grout, slipping like a pale snake into her mouth, forcing open her throat, coiling in a pile in her gut—

"No," Aimee says. "No, I can't."

"Sweetheart, what do you mean you can't?" Her mother's face is getting that look of anguished pleading that makes Aimee want to shut her eyes and scream.

"I just can't."

"Well I may have to put my foot down here."

"No!"

"The book said you might resist going to the doctor, but I'm supposed to be firm and say that I'm the adult here, I'm going to do this for your own good and—"

"Stop talking to me about what you read in some stupid book! You're always saying you want me to act like an adult but it's so obvious that it doesn't even matter to you what I want—"

"It does matter, it does matter to me what you want, it's just that sometimes what a person wants isn't what's best for them, can you understand that?"

"You're such a liar!" Aimee screams, losing it now. "You're a hypocritical liar!"

From downstairs comes the sound, distant but distinct, of Aimee's mother's cell phone ringing: a high-pitched synth version of some upbeat classical piece. This cell phone almost never rings, because the only people who ever call it are her mom's work people, and Aimee's mom is almost always at work when the work people need her.

"Oh crap!" Her mother's manicured hand flies up to cover her mouth too late to keep the mild curse from escaping. She looks down at her watch, wild-eyed, then back at her daughter. "Midmonth meeting," she says, panicked.

Aimee nods as if she knows what this means. The phone starts over at the beginning of its plinkety tune—only half a plinkety tune left before it kicks over to voice mail.

"Get it," Aimee orders authoritatively, and her mother takes the command as if Aimee were her boss, flying out of the room and down the carpeted stairs to where the phone is buried in her purse by the front door.

"Hello?" Aimee hears her answer breathlessly, having caught the call just in the nick of time. "Paul? Yes I am, I am *out* the door, I'm just dealing with a little situation here at home."

Aimee slumps back onto the bed, her floor-bruised hips and shoulders murmuring achy complaints as she moves. After just a moment her mother reappears, bracing herself with both hands against the doorframe like a drunken cowboy in a saloon. The morning perfection of eight minutes ago has already been violated—her hair has redistributed itself unevenly around her head and one side of her blouse is boiling over the waistband of her skirt.

"I can't believe I have to do this," her mother says hoarsely, "because you just said some quite rude things to me that I'd like to respond to, and as you know I don't like to interrupt a Conversation in the middle. But I forgot that it's midmonth meeting morning and I absolutely have to go in to the office right now. But we are going to pick this Conversation up right where we left it when I get home."

Aimee shrugs and looks away.

"In the meantime you know the drill. Medicines in the medicine cabinet, tea above the stove, minimal TV, please, and I'll try to make it home early."

"Okay." Aimee still doesn't look at her mother.

"I love you," her mother apologizes.

Aimee flushes with embarrassment, staring at the wall. When she turns back to look at the doorway, her mother is gone.

After lying perfectly still for ten minutes, waiting to make sure that the Toyota doesn't change its mind and pull back into the driveway, Aimee springs to life.

She puts her favorite all-velvet outfit together, shoves her notebook and a couple of recently printed-out poems into her army satchel, and heads for the municipal bus stop at the entrance to Riverglade Estates.

• • •

The English Department at the university is located in a building called Chancellor's Hall—that much Aimee remembers. Other than the odd mention of its name, however, Bill never talked much about his office. Whenever Aimee used to picture where Bill worked she imagined a stately granite building, kind of a cross between a library and a bank, with columns and cornices and a couple of stone lions and maybe a bronze statue of some literary hero out front: Shakespeare with his little mustache and puffy shorts, considering his quill. Aimee used to imagine Bill jogging up a grand flight of stone steps every morning, briefcase in hand and arms full of books, pulling open the rich mahogany door with its iron handle and entering the hushed marble vault of the vestibule, alive with the echoes of scholars old and young whispering lines of verse to one another in the corridors overhead.

In reality, Chancellor's Hall turns out to be a long cement Kleenex box of a building, covered with stucco the color of stained teeth, with warping aqua blue vinyl panels set in beneath each of its narrow gray windows. The main doors, half blocked by a bike rack buried in a heap of bikes, flutter with a fringe of multicolored fliers that have been taped one on top of the other to cover every available square inch of plate glass.

It has taken Aimee almost half an hour to find Chancellor's Hall since she located it on the scratchiti-covered map posted near the bus shelter where she got off. The university's campus seems to her so far like a maze of almost identical buildings, some of them squat and some of them tall but all of them ugly and none of them granite. In the half an hour she has spent wandering the place, she hasn't seen a single literary statue or stone lion, just a lot of dazed-looking college students meandering around in twos and threes, uniformed in nearly identical hoodies and jeans, wearing nearly identical backpacks and baseball caps. Most of them could pass for Valley Regional kids, except for the fact that about half of them are casually smoking cigarettes.

Aimee stands for a second in front of the flapping neon-bright fliers. Apparently a movie from 1963 about a blonde chick running away from the police is being shown this evening in French. A class called "The Economics of Post-Colonial Africa" is being offered for three credits, taught by a guy named R. F. P. Naroyan. Someone has lost her cat, Derek Whiskerton III, and will pay a "huge reward" to whoever returns him safely to her; the cat glowers out of its photocopied portrait like a cat of the dead, pupils white with flash. Two guys are looking for a roommate to share an off-campus apartment with, preferably female, "must love to party!!!"

"Ex*cuse* us?"

Aimee turns. A pair of ponytailed girls, virtually indistinguishable from one another in matching university pullovers and sweatpants, waistbands rolled down to reveal matching strips of orange-tanned stomach, have come giggling up behind her as she zoned out in front of the fliers.

"Can we, like, get through here?"

Aimee steps aside, moving her mouth in the shape of "sorry," though no voice comes out.

When the Ponytails yank open the door, murmuring to each other, Aimee follows them through it, into a lobby that is in every way the opposite of a hushed marble vestibule. Low ceilings, no windows, black vinyl flooring, banks of greenish fluorescent lights that hum a sickly harmony with the drone of a huge glowing Coke machine that dominates the space. The Ponytails flounce off down a corridor and Aimee stands alone for a second, taking in the massive disappointment of Chancellor's Hall. It's quiet, but in a dull, stressed-out way, the quiet of a doctor's office or cheap hotel, not the rich quiet of a hall of learning.

Aimee finds a directory on the wall by the Coke machine—the kind of black signboard with plastic letters stuck in it that they use to post the specials on in rest-stop diners—and runs down the list of names until she finds Bill's. His office number is 104. She sets out down the same hallway the Ponytails disappeared into.

The door to room 104 is smooth, featureless wood with a 3 x 5 index card taped to the middle that reads, in block capital ballpoint-pen letters:

DR. WILLIAM PRUFER
GREAT WORKS/POETRY I/FRESHMAN COMP
OFFICE HOURS BY APPOINTMENT

Aimee knocks at the center of the index card twice: *rap rap.*

"Take a number!" Bill yells from inside.

The sound of girls' laughter filters through the door. Aimee knocks again: *rap rap rap.*

"I said take a *number!*"

The door swings open and Aimee looks down into Bill's up-turned, upside-down face. He's reclined way back in his chair so he can reach the doorknob without getting up, and he's practically horizontal. But when he sees Aimee he sits bolt upright and turns around to face her.

"What are you doing here?" Bill doesn't even pretend to be glad to see her.

"I . . ." Aimee wants to explain, but she's overwhelmed by the powerful wave of Bill-ness that's pouring through the open door. The cramped, windowless office she catches a glimpse of behind Bill is saturated with the smell of him—part spicy aftershave, part used bookstore, part stale memory of cigarettes—and the painfully familiar scent knocks out Aimee's coherence like a baseball smashing out a porch light.

"I've got students here," Bill says when Aimee doesn't finish her sentence. He opens the door wider to reveal the Ponytails huddled up together on a small couch against the far wall.

"We were here first?" one of them says, extending a challenge.

"No, yeah, I'll wait."

"Well . . . I don't know if you want to do that. I have a lot of people coming in today, boom boom boom, one right after the other. I don't know if it makes sense for you to wait."

Aimee just stands there.

"It's almost midterms, see, Ame. I didn't know you were gonna show up, I would have told you not to come."

Aimee's heart starts a slow, familiar descent.

"Can I just . . . five minutes, Bill?"

Bill sighs.

"Five minutes, as soon as I'm done with these two. Even though they don't know the first thing about T. S. Eliot"—Bill turns to the Ponytails and winks at them—they giggle—"I'll do my best to make it quick."

"I'll wait. I won't go anywhere."

Bill nods and closes his door with a clunk.

Aimee stands there for a second, nose to nose with the index card on Bill's door. Mechanically she turns around, leans back against the wall beside 104, and lowers herself inch by inch to the floor. Her heart continues its slow, oozing slide down her center on its way to the pit of her stomach.

As the minutes tick by, kids start ambling up to Bill's door, bashful and aloof, not talking to each other. It's a weirder sample of kids, in general, than the ones Aimee was seeing out around campus—there's a giantly tall blond guy with big glasses and an enormous Adam's apple, a short kid with an Afro, carrying a guitar case, a girl with dyed black hair and Doc Martens who eyes Aimee and her black-velvet-and-combat-boots ensemble with a mixture of recognition and suspicion.

After a little while, Aimee realizes that the giantly tall guy keeps looking at her. Little furtive looks, always looking away before she can meet his eye. He focuses his eyes on the ceiling and, as if he's following a map to Aimee's side printed on the acoustic tiles up there, he moves awkwardly to stand beside her. His Twinkie-yellow hair hangs in a limp flop across his forehead and his cheeks are ravaged with angry red acne. Suddenly, as if he's received a silent cue, he drops to the floor next to Aimee and starts folding himself up like a huge collapsible lawn chair. His arms and legs seem to bend in three or four different places as he packs himself down into a compact position. After maybe thirty seconds of complicated sitting down, he looks straight at Aimee. He's on the verge of saying hello to her when the door to 104 opens at last and the Ponytails come out, giggling to each other like they just heard a great piece of gossip.

Bill's curly head emerges next; it swivels around until he finds Aimee.

"Zorn," he says, pointing at her. "Next."

Inside the closet-sized office Bill points to the little couch and Aimee sits.

"So," he says, lapsing into his chair, "make it snappy."

Make it snappy?

What Aimee wants to say to Bill would take hours. It would take days. It would take so many hours and so many days that really the simplest thing would be for Bill to just move back into the house so she could have all the access to him she needs, to tell him everything she needs to tell him.

"Bill," says Aimee.

There he is, real live Bill, looking at her expectantly, brown curls and brown dog eyes and raspy unshaven face. Aimee realizes that in the weeks since he left she's already forgotten so many physical details about Bill, so many tiny wrinkles and sags and hairs on his face and body that she used to be aware of—they've been slowly getting wiped off her mental image of him. Her memory of Bill has become an Impressionist portrait, broad brushstrokes that only form an image from a distance. The reality of him is blazing with exquisite detail—she almost can't bear to take him all in.

Looking at Bill, she misses him unbearably, even though he's right in front of her.

"What's up, Ame? What brings you down here in person? You jonesing to talk about great works of modern literature?"

"Um, I was hoping you would give me some advice. It is partly about poetry, though."

"Shoot."

"Bill." Aimee takes a deep breath. "What would you do if a girl that you were sort of friends with but not really took this poem that you wrote and kind of stole it but not exactly and won this prize with it and everybody thought she was a genius but really it was you that was kind of the genius, and also there was this other girl who could maybe help you get the poem back but she was hugely weird and scary in a bunch of different ways and you didn't know if you should ask her for help because she might turn out to be even weirder up close than from far away. But still it seemed like she might be the only one who could help you get your poem back, what would you do?"

Bill shakes his head out like a dizzy cartoon character. "Wait, who? Who could help you get the poem back?"

"The weird girl."

"Honestly, Ame, I can't tell how many girls you've got in this story, and which of them are weird and which aren't and . . ." Bill trails off, looks around his office as if searching for a clue as to how to carry on. "Something tells me I'd have to get like an hour's worth of backstory to really grasp what you're talking about and frankly, I don't have an hour to spare for backstory. So let's cut to the chase here. Clearly there's some major thing going on in your life right now, some kind of major emotional event going down in some kind of major emotional way. And it sounds like you need someone to take care of you a little."

"I don't need anyone to take care of me." Aimee straightens her spine.

"There's no shame in it, man. Everybody needs someone to take care of them, especially kids. I mean, what are you, twelve?"

"I'm *fourteen*, Bill."

"Right, you're just a little tiny kid who needs someone to look out for you sometimes."

First Aimee feels embarrassed by this, then violently annoyed. But in the middle of those dark, swirling feelings she also feels a tiny spark of hope ignite—is Bill about to offer to take care of her? Maybe Bill's about to tell her that she can move in with him in his new bachelor pad in Maple Park, the subdivision out behind the university.

And in a split-second Aimee imagines the whole thing: abandoning her dumb, boring, pointless room and her dumb, boring, nervous mom, shoving her six poetry notebooks and her three velvet hats and her sandalwood candle into her satchel and walking away from Riverglade Estates without even turning to wave back at her mom as she strides off down the cul-de-sac. Showing up at Bill's place, ringing the doorbell and bouncing on her toes as she waits for him to open the door and beckon her in. She can just picture how Bill must have "decorated" his crummy new apartment, with a crummy futon and a crummy Ikea coffee table and cheap crummy Christmas lights taped to the wall up by the ceiling, and books, books—books in stacks on either side of the front door and books spilling out from under the futon, a stack of books holding up the TV, a stack of books pressing down the TV, so many books that they've taken over the kitchen and there's not even any room left for food, so that when you reach into a kitchen cabinet looking for, say, oatmeal you pull out *The Complete Works of William Blake* instead. Aimee imagines Bill staying up late with her every night arguing about who's a more significant writer, Frank O'Hara or William Burroughs. She imagines Bill letting her sleep on the crummy futon, and meeting her every day after school at the kitchen table like he used to, and eating Jell-O with her like he used to, and making jokes with her like he used to. She imagines her whole life turning out basically perfect from now on.

"I don't know, maybe," Aimee says, angling. "I guess maybe I do need someone to take care of me. . . ."

"Well it's very mature of you to recognize that," Bill says, nodding gravely. "And it just so happens that you are extremely tight with someone who's aces at taking care of people. You know who I'm referring to?"

Aimee looks up at him questioningly, shaking her head. *You?* she thinks. *You, you, you?*

"Kathy Zorn!" Bill spreads his big hands out—*tada!*—like he's just revealed the punch line to a supersmart joke.

For a second Aimee doesn't even recognize the name.

"Who?" she asks.

Bill leans forward and biffs Aimee lightly on the knee.

"Your mom, goofbat," he says, grinning.

"*What?*"

"Have you even told her that there's something going on with you? Dollars to doughnuts you haven't told her a thing."

"No way, no way, there's no *way* I'd ever talk to her about any of this. She doesn't understand a word I say."

"I know you think that, but I think you're wrong."

"Come on, Bill, she's an idiot. *You* know that."

"Excuse me?" Bill's expression darkens and he pulls away, sits back hard in his chair. "You think *I* think your mother's an idiot?"

"Well you left her, didn't you?"

Bill's mouth drops open.

"Well, I mean—yeah, but . . ."

Bill looks away from Aimee, grips his jaw with his hand, and sort of kneads the lower half of his face. His mouth opens, closes. Even during his worst fights with her mom, Aimee never saw him at a loss for words.

"Look, Ame," he begins at last, his voice low and searching. "I can't explain why two people with practically nothing in common would ever fall in love in the first place, and I can't explain why they'd stay together, or why they'd break up. Love is a mystery, man, I'm sure they covered that in school already. But you can't be walking around thinking that your mom and I broke up because somehow I don't respect her as a human being."

Bill's gaze as he peers into Aimee's face to say this is so raw and sincere that she has to look away.

"I don't know if you know this about me, but when your mom first met me I was a serious mess, I was nothing but a drunken doofus, I wasn't worth a dog's spit on the sidewalk, and your mom saw something worth saving in me. She believed that I could be a decent human being, and even though basically on some level she was wrong, basically on some level I'm always going to be a drunken doofus, that wasn't her fault. I think when I was living with you guys I came closer to being a decent human being than I'm ever likely to be again."

"I don't know what you're talking about," Aimee says, mortified.

"What I'm saying is *talk* to your mother, man! She's a genius at building people up and making them feel better, that's like her main skill in life. And there she is, right there in your house—she's a resource, Ame, use her!"

"I don't want to use her, I want to use *you*."

"God no—me? You've got to be kidding."

"You're the only one who understands me, Bill!"

The sentence comes ribboning out of Aimee before she has time to think better of it, but once it's out, billowing in the air between them, Aimee feels shattered by the lonely truth of it. And by the hideously embarrassing fact that she said it out loud.

Like a sudden summer downpour, Aimee begins to cry.

"Okay, Ame, now please don't freak. Don't wig out on me now, I've got office hours here."

Aimee sniffles, wipes her nose with the back of her hand. As she pulls it together they both look away, up at the bookshelves lining the walls of the tiny space, rather than looking directly at each other.

"Listen, Ame. Besides all the obvious reasons why I'm no good for you as a confidant, the main problem is that I've already got between eighty and a hundred and twenty kids a semester who need me to take care of them and hold their hands and dry their tears and solve all their freaking problems. And believe me, they are *way* more messed up than you, my friend. Those last two in here—the Piggytail Twins, I call them—they are absolutely convinced that 'The Love Song of J. Alfred Prufrock' by T. S. Eliot is a horror story about a werewolf."

Aimee laughs a little, through the last of her tears.

"Crazy, right?" Bill grins at her, encouraged. "The whole time you were out in the hall I'm going, show me this alleged werewolf. What the hell makes you think this lyrical meditation on the alienation of modern man is about a freaking werewolf? No werewolf in the *entire* poem. They've *both* written me ten-page papers about T. S. Eliot and his world-famous werewolf. You'd never make a mistake like that, Ame, right? You're way ahead of the game. You just need a little backup. So if you're not going to talk to your mom, I think you should talk to the weird girl. Weird is good. Weird is promising. Some of my best friends are weirdos." Bill pauses. "All of them, actually. Everybody I ever loved is weird as hell."

"But Mom's the opposite of weird. You loved her."

Bill smiles a sad smile, the last one Aimee will see for a long time.

"I did," he says. "I do. The exception that proves the rule."

• 15 •

Wednesday, double B Period: Double Brit Lit. Auditorium. Performance Project.

Out in the audience somewhere, hidden from Meghan's view but snickering audibly, are J-Bar and his crew. They arrived en masse five minutes after the bell, sauntered through the main auditorium doors in their ringer Ts and tablecloth togas and took their sweet time coming down the aisle, making a big show of barely giving a damn.

"Coach said we could come," J-Bar explained to Mr. Handsley when he reached the first row of seats, just to remind him who the important teacher was.

"Welcome," Mr. Handsley said tightly, and didn't even acknowledge their lateness, just kept going over the order of the *Caesar* scenes, which exotic-fruit group would be performing when.

Now, in the dusty dark of backstage, Becky Trainer is beside Meghan, breathing shallowly in her bedsheet toga, watching as

Martha Scherpa and Kaitlyn Carmigan prep for their big debut on stage.

"I'll give the cue," Becky whispers to Meghan. "When all of the Papayas are at places, I'll say 'places,' and when it's time for you to pull the curtain I'll say 'curtain.'"

Meghan nods.

"Did you get that?" Becky raises her eyebrows. "'Places,' and then 'curtain.' And then you pull the curtain."

I get it, Meghan thinks, *because I am neither deaf nor brain damaged.* She nods again.

"Okay. Okay, then." Becky looks unconvinced, but she turns to shade her eyes with her hand and squint toward the stage, where Martha and Kaitlyn seem to be having a whispered fight in the half-light about where to place the foam acting cube. Martha points right and Kaitlyn shakes her head vigorously and points left.

"God, Papayas," Becky hisses, "we said two feet upstage of the yellow spike tape, it's *so, extremely, simple!*" She marches onstage, clutching the place at her shoulder where her bedsheet is pinned precariously together, and begins to boss Kaitlyn and Martha in a silent tantrum.

Alone in the dark Meghan relaxes. She exhales and realizes that she had been holding her breath the whole time Becky was beside her. The rope for the curtain feels good in her hands, rough and bristly and powerful—almost alive—and she runs her palms up and down it, losing herself in the feeling a little.

Behind her, a little adenoidal voice mutters, "Friends Romans countrymen lend me your ears I come to bury Caesar not to praise him friends Romans countrymen lend me your ears I come to bury Caesar not to praise him . . ."

Meghan turns to look at Jonah Boyd, a badger in a bedsheet, scuttling around in a circle with his hands clasped behind his back about ten feet away. His greasy hair is slicked down like a dictator's in a slab across his forehead, and his toga is fastened over a boldly striped turtleneck. He looks up in the middle of pacing, meets Meghan's eye, and halts.

"Can I help you?" he asks skeptically.

Meghan gives her head a single shake no.

"I'm aware that I'm not in the next scene, if that's why you're looking at me like that, but I prefer to wait for my turn here instead of down in the audience. I'm delivering the crucial Mark Antony speech, in which he convinces the crowd to mourn the murdered Caesar and turn against Brutus and the conspirators. It's the most famous passage of the play. It's a masterpiece of rhetoric. I'm extremely nervous."

Meghan almost smiles.

"Kindly don't watch me while I practice my lines."

Obediently Meghan turns back to her post—and comes face to face with Aimee Zorn, standing not six inches away from her.

Meghan's heart stutters.

She staggers back a step.

"Hey," whispers Aimee. "There you are."

Overwhelmed, Meghan looks away. Out onstage Becky's sign-language abuse of her scene mates has escalated into huge, acrobatic gestures of frustration.

"I've been looking everywhere for you. First you stalk me like a creepy stalker and then I can't find you anywhere."

Wildly Meghan casts her eyes around the space, searching for any-place to look but at Aimee Zorn. For a moment she stares up into the murk of the flyspace, wishing she could shrink to the size of a dust mote, float up into the dark, and disappear.

"Okay, you don't have to talk to me," Aimee says quietly. "Just listen. I need your help."

Meghan turns, slowly, and lets herself look at Aimee. It's not an honest face. It's not a kind face. It's a face made of anger and secrets and lies. From the tight, guarded mouth to the clenched, square jaw to the glossy shimmer of I-dare-you-to that coats the surface of her eyes, Aimee's face is a scary place for Meghan's gaze to rest. But beneath the gloss, beneath the sharpness and tension, deep at Aimee's core, Meghan can see something warm and real. It's the same unnameable thing she saw in the sickroom on the first day of school. It's the same thing she feels pulsing softly deep in her own chest.

"What do you need?" Meghan asks.

"Didn't you hear me?" Becky Trainer explodes into Meghan's periphery. "I said 'places' like four hundred times!"

Aimee drops back into the darkness, leaving Meghan alone. Startled and confused, Meghan lurches toward the curtain rope, grabs it with both hands, and starts to pull.

"Not 'curtain,'" Becky whisper-screeches, "'places,' I said 'places'! I *knew* you didn't get it the first time!"

"I *get* it," Meghan says loudly and clearly, and the sound of her voice coming out of her own mouth, here, in the middle of a public place, is such a rare, freakish occurrence that it takes even her by surprise. Becky Trainer pauses for a second and regards Meghan curiously.

"Sorry," she says with a kind of awe. "Are you . . . ready to do the curtain now?"

Meghan nods and hauls the rope down, hand-over-hand, with all her strength. Out onstage the thick orange drape splits apart and heaves in two directions, dragging along the dusty stage as it retreats with a clacking sound into the wings. The stage is flooded with brilliant light.

After a moment's frozen tableau, one foot propped on the acting cube like a statue, Martha Scherpa raises her arm in an awkward salute.

"Another general shout!" she yells, clearly projecting from the diaphragm as Becky has instructed her to. "I do believe that these applauses are for some new honours that are heap'd on Caesar."

At this Becky Trainer leaves Meghan's side and strides out onstage, still clutching her untrustworthy shoulder seam.

"Why, man," she bellows in a gruff baritone, "he doth bestride the narrow world like a Colossus, and we petty men walk under his huge legs. . . . The fault, dear Brutus, is not in our stars but in ourselves, that we are underlings."

"It's Cara." From behind Meghan, Aimee's voice comes, hushed and cool.

"I told you so."

Aimee comes to stand next to Meghan. "Harsh," she says.

"That's harsh?" Meghan whispers. "Kind of like calling someone sick and disgusting?"

Aimee is silent for a second.

"Sorry," she says.

"Yeah." Meghan nods to herself, as if she's calling it up from memory now: "Sick, and disgusting. And you said you were gonna call the police on me."

"Well you followed me to my house!"

"So?"

"That's a really weird thing to do!"

"I wanted to tell you something, but you didn't want to listen."

Again, Aimee's quiet.

"Sorry," she says again.

Out onstage Kaitlyn Carmigan, Madison Beam, and McKenzie Kirby-Kozak come tromping on in regal formation, drawing Meghan's attention.

"Caesar!" shouts Madison. Meghan notices that Madison's toga has tiny little pastel sailboats all over it. Becky must have flipped when she showed up in that thing.

"So what did she do?" Meghan whispers after a second.

"I . . . it's too complicated to explain right now."

"Okay." Meghan pauses. "Basic nature of the crime?"

"Theft," Aimee replies in Meghan's ear. "Betrayal."

Meghan nods. She won't say *I told you so* twice.

Out onstage Becky drops with a thunk to her knees. The other Papayas scurry to surround her in a hyper-dramatic modern dance pose, fingers undulating in a frame around her head, as Becky hollers out into the void of the auditorium, "And after this let Caesar seat him sure, for we will shake him, or worse days endure."

Becky drops her head tragically and all five girls freeze with their hands spread around her.

From the auditorium, an anticlimactic smattering of applause, like stray drips of water splattering from a leaky faucet. Meghan can picture J-Bar and his crew, each sprawled out across three or four flip-down seats in their togas and Air Jordans, slapping their hands together in sarcastic ovation.

Onstage Becky breaks her perfect scene-closing stillness to turn her chin in Meghan's direction and hiss through her teeth, *"Curtain!"*

Hastily Meghan grabs the far loop of the rope and hauls it down, closing the curtain and plunging backstage into inky darkness again.

The Papayas mill excitedly offstage in the opposite direction, and through the curtain Meghan hears Mr. Handsley yell, "Persimmons, up!"

Now Meghan turns back to Aimee again. "What'd she steal?"

Aimee looks a little sheepish, like what she's about to say hasn't quite been worth so much buildup. She looks down before she says, "Um. My poem."

"Like, out of your locker?"

"No, it's, um, she sort of . . . copied my poem, and submitted it to this competition, and won, and I want it back."

"You mean like, you want the paper back?"

"No, I want the *words* back, I want the *idea* back. I don't want people thinking it's her idea."

Meghan nods for a second, thinking that over. "It's not that hard to steal ideas," she observes, "but it's really hard to steal them back."

A commotion onstage—someone's trying to beat their way through the curtain. Meghan reaches up and reels it open a foot, and the Persimmons stride through the gap in single file: Freedom, Zach Mishra, Shane, and J-Bar, shouldering the curtain aside as they pass through it and snickering to each other as they go.

Onstage they huddle up, reviewing their game plan. Then they join hands in the center and break with a quiet grunt. J-Bar splits from the group and saunters toward Meghan. She steels herself, feels herself shrinking away from him inside her body even though she's not moving an inch.

J-Bar waits until he's half a foot away from Meghan before he speaks.

"Hey, Butter Ball," he says, muted as a golf announcer. "You're looking so fine today I could just lick you from your—"

Beside her Meghan feels Aimee take a step forward, emerging from the shadows into bold, sudden visibility. For a split second J-Bar's face registers shock and embarrassment, then he switches modes smoothly, with no hesitation—he's all business now that he sees that he and Meghan aren't alone.

"Um so can you open the curtain when I give this signal?" He demonstrates a vertical cutting motion in the air. Meghan nods. "And can you close it after Freedom says 'Then fall, Caesar'?" Meghan nods again. "Cool. Thanks," J-Bar says tonelessly, and he turns and rejoins the other Persimmons.

There's a silence. Meghan can't look at Aimee. She waits for Aimee to ask, "What was that about?" She waits for Aimee to ask, "What was he about to say to you?" She waits for Aimee to disappear.

But Aimee says nothing, and Meghan says nothing. Nobody goes. They just stand there side by side, looking out onstage, not speaking.

After what feels like a very long time Aimee says quietly, "Mutant."

And for the first time in what feels like months, Meghan smiles.

Within seconds of their scene beginning, Meghan realizes with mounting pleasure that the jocks are doing a terrible job.

Shane is standing stock still, his bony shoulders sticking out of either side of his toga, his arms hanging stiffly as two wooden walking sticks by his sides. Beneath his bedsheet his bare legs are a skeleton's legs with hair. Freedom, who prowls like a panther in gym class and struts like a pimp in the halls—nothing but swagger—has an animatronic quality onstage, shuffling into place and then freezing, lock-jawed and brain dead. Even J-Bar, sultan of suave, moves haltingly out there, like a deer caught in headlights. And he's mumbling. They're all mumbling—no one can hear a word they're saying.

"Man, they suck," Aimee says quietly at Meghan's shoulder.

"Speak up!" Mr. Handsley barks from the audience.

"DothnotBrutusbootlesskneel," mumbles J-Bar.

"I said speak *up*! Try that line again, young J-Bar!" Mr. Handsley's voice is getting louder—he's approaching the stage.

"DothnotBrutusbootlesskneel." J-Bar gums the words like a toothless old guy biting at a sandwich.

"So, um, listen," Aimee whispers, "the thing is that there's kind of a time thing, it's kind of urgent, I kind of need your help right now.

So can we meet up sometime kind of soon to make a plan?"

As much as Meghan wants to pay attention to Aimee, she can't tear her eyes off the sight of J-Bar suffering in front of the entire class. Even from this far away she can see a sheen of sweat forming on his golden forehead. His mouth is twitching and his eyes are dark and full of storms. This isn't easy for him, and he isn't having a good time.

"Um . . ." Meghan whispers to Aimee distractedly. "Today after school?"

"Perfect. Where?"

"Louder!" Mr. Handsley cries, and vaults suddenly from the orchestra pit up onto the stage, a stunningly athletic move from this man whom Meghan has only ever seen taking small, precise steps around a classroom.

"This is the *murder* scene!" Mr. Handsley cries. "This is the *betrayal* scene, this is arguably the crux of the entire play and it is certainly a challenging moment of physical stagecraft, which is why I assigned it to you Persimmons, mindful of your well-known talent for things physical. And here you are standing around like mannequins, muttering into your chests—you're breaking my heart! Let's see a little *action*, let's see a little *animation*! Let's hear a little *projection* out of you! Take it from 'That I was constant Cimber should be banish'd.'"

Mr. Handsley steps back but doesn't leave the stage. J-Bar takes in a sharp, strangled breath and mutters, "ThatIwasconstantCimber shouldbebanish'dand—"

"Stop, stop, stop!" Mr. Handsley grips his head dramatically with both hands. "I'm sorry, I can't let you go on like that. First of all, how does an emperor stand?" He gets right up in J-Bar's face—or as close to J-Bar's face as he can get, given that the six-foot-two basketball captain towers over him. "Does an emperor stand like this, like a robot on steroids?" Mr. Handsley turns out to face the audience and apes J-Bar's posture, slouched over, shoulders hunched. Then he whirls around to face Freedom. "And you, Mr. Falcon—does a noble Roman conspirator stand like this?" He imitates Freedom's strait-jacketed stance. "Come on, now, Persimmons, you're supposed to be young Olympians. Let's see some physical *theater* out of you gentlemen!"

Mr. Handsley jogs off to the side again. The Persimmons look at each other dolefully and shuffle back into the same lifeless configuration they were in before their teacher interrupted them.

"So, um . . ." Aimee taps Meghan's shoulder lightly. "The bell's gonna ring soon and I just—where do you want to meet today?"

"ThatIwasconstantCimbershouldbebanish'd," J-Bar mumbles onstage.

"Louder," prompts Mr. Handsley.

"O Caesar!" Shane howls.

"Better!" shouts Mr. Handsley.

"HencewiltthouliftupOlympus—" J-Bar grunts.

"Mr. Bartlett, no no no and no!"

"What about my house?" Meghan says absently, not able to look away from the riveting scene onstage.

"Great, yeah, where's that?" Aimee asks.

"Speak from *here*"—Mr. Handsley claps his palm to J-Bar's

bedsheet-wrapped abdomen—"not from *here.*" He slaps J-Bar's broad chest with his open palm. J-Bar flinches but Mr. Handsley doesn't let up. "*This* is the source of the emperor's voice!" He goes to put his hand on J-Bar's stomach again but J-Bar takes a step back.

"Don't touch me," J-Bar mutters, threateningly serious.

"*Hey,*" Aimee says loudly in Meghan's ear.

Meghan manages to tear her eyes off the deconstruction of J-Bar and turns to look at Aimee.

"Why don't we meet at the old barn, you know where that is?" she asks Aimee.

"I said *quit* it!" J-Bar shouts, a real, ragged shout—uncontrolled and full of emotion.

Meghan whips back around only to see Mr. Handsley sprawled out flat on his back and J-Bar running toward the edge of the stage. Without breaking stride he leaps off into the blackness, toga billowing around him like a cape, and disappears.

It dawns on Meghan instantly: *Something huge just took place, something that will change the future of Valley Regional High. And I was looking away when it happened.*

For a long, fractured second nobody moves. Then, hesitantly, Mr. Handsley begins to stand up, getting first to his knees, then hauling himself laboriously to his feet, brushing dirt and sawdust off his trousers and sleeves.

"Persimmons, thank you for your work. Take five," he says quietly to the remaining thespians. Sedately he crosses the stage and trots down the steps to the pit, following J-Bar but not chasing him.

Shane says something out of the side of his mouth and the left-over Persimmons wander aimlessly away, jumping off the lip of the stage and dispersing individually into the darkness.

More than anything else right now, Meghan wishes she could be wherever J-Bar and Mr. Handsley are. The confrontation that's going down between them right now must be so juicy, so unbelievable—all she wants to do is leave Aimee here in the dark and go find out where J-Bar went when he ran.

"So you were saying we should meet at the barn?" Aimee prompts, trying to get Meghan's attention. "You mean the one that's out near my house, in the middle of the cornfield?"

"Yeah, that one. It's near my house, too."

"Oh, you live out there?"

Meghan nods. "Meet me there at four thirty?"

"Cool."

The bell rings—a distant echo of a bell here, deep in the cave of the auditorium.

"Um, wait," Aimee calls after her as Meghan turns to leave. "Can I ask you one more thing?"

"Sure."

"Um, can you tell me your name?"

Meghan's already overfull heart constricts and spills sloppily over the sides. She can't remember the last time she spoke her name out loud.

"Meghan," she says.

"Hey. I'm Aimee."

"Yeah," says Meghan Ball. "I know."

• 16 •

When Aimee gets off Bus 12, the Toyota is parked at the edge of the cul-de-sac. Her mother's home early from work. Naturally, since Aimee got into bed and turned off the light at six P.M. last night to preempt another Conversation, her mother has taken a half day today—of all days—to make sure it happens now.

In the kitchen her mother has clearly been waiting for her, leaning up against the counter in half-undone work clothes and flip-flops, with a bright, fake-relaxed expression on her face, sipping a Diet Coke.

Aimee decides to make things easy on both of them and match her mother's mood. "Hi!" she says, chipper as a cheerleader. "You're home early!"

Her mother smiles and nods, but eyes Aimee with mild suspicion.

"That's right, I am. I thought we could spend the afternoon together," she offers. "Finish up our Conversation from the other day."

"Oh, um, that sounds great, I really wish I could, but I promised . . . my friend I'd meet her this afternoon. I didn't know you were gonna be home early."

"Cara?" her mother asks with genuine eagerness. "You're meeting Cara?"

Aimee swallows.

"Yeah," she says.

"Well why don't you and me sit down and have a snack together, just for a couple of minutes, and then I'll drive you over to her house."

"Well . . . actually I'm supposed to meet her right now. She's waiting for me."

"Okay, I'll drive you right now. We can talk in the car."

"Thanks, Mom, that's so nice, but I can walk."

"To Albemarle Road? That's nuts, it'll take you hours."

"I'm not—we're not—I'm not going to—"

Right now, as her mother stands there in front of her desperately trying to do the right thing, Aimee wants to tell her the whole story from beginning to end, from the first moment Cara burst into her life, perfect and glittering, all the way up to this afternoon, when Cara's gone and she's about to go meet the most despised girl in school, a girl made of mud and cellulite, in the ruins of an abandoned barn. She hears Bill's voice in her mind: "She's a resource, Ame, use her!" She sees her mother's open, pleading look, practically begging her to tell her what's going on. Aimee takes a breath to tell her the truth, but something catches in her throat.

"We're not meeting at her house," Aimee explains feebly. "We're meeting in the woods. Out in back of Riverglade."

Her mother's expression clouds over with confusion.

"To do some nature writing," Aimee adds hurriedly.

Her mother's face clears.

"How wonderful," says her mom. "How creative." Her mother's eyes fill with that clear yearning that makes Aimee want to look away, that open, watery wish that Aimee will somehow manage to be okay. It's awful to lie to your mother when she's looking at you like that. Aimee hangs her head; this is shame.

"Sweetheart, can I tell you why I like this girl? It's not just because she seems like she must be a very nice person, although she does seem like she must be a very nice person. I like this girl because she's supportive of your poetry writing, and I know how important your poetry writing is to you. I'm so proud of you for working so hard on it. And you know who else would be proud if he knew you were sticking with it is Bill."

Shame, shame, shame.

"You should call him sometime and let him know what you're up to." Aimee's mother is speaking carefully now, as if she's rehearsed this speech several times in her head. "I want you to know that it's okay with me if you stay in touch with him. I know that you two had a special connection and I don't want that to disappear just because Bill and I didn't work out. You shouldn't have to lose him as a friend just because he's not with us anymore."

He's not dead, thinks Aimee, *he's living in a bachelor pad in Maple Park.* Aimee wonders if her mother read an article on this in one of her magazines, or saw a segment about it on *Oprah*: How to Help Your Kids Stay Friends with Your Ex-Boyfriend—Even When You Hate His Guts!

"Okay," Aimee says, nodding, trying to look like the idea is just occurring to her, "maybe I'll call him again sometime. Just to say hi."

Her mother nods and smiles sadly, and Aimee wonders suddenly if she said the wrong thing, if she was supposed to say, *No, no, I would never call Bill—I don't need him, I only need you.* But it's too late, she's said what she's said.

"You are a very special, very talented girl," her mother says now, lifting off the counter where she's been propped and taking a couple of tentative steps toward Aimee. "Bill always told me that you were something special. Not that I needed him to tell me that, but I mean his expert opinion was that you were a gifted girl. And I know that if you put your mind to it and keep working hard, you can be a writer when you grow up. If that's what you want."

Flushed with embarrassment, Aimee nods a straggly nod. She doesn't know whether she should say something to make this stop or just keep quiet and let her mother run out of steam.

"I'll always be proud of you, no matter what," her mother says. "And I need you to know that I'll do anything I can to help you if you're having a problem. Any kind of problem at all."

Her eyes fill up with the beginnings of tears, and she reaches out and lays her hand on Aimee's arm. Aimee freezes under the weight of the wooden touch. Her mother's palm is damp with Coke-can sweat and it just lies there, inert, on Aimee's numb forearm. They stand there for a moment, locked in that position, like two marionettes trying to bring each other to life.

After a moment her mother sighs a brief sigh, retracts her hand, and turns back to the counter. Aimee can see her pulling herself together, tidying herself mentally, like a sped-up film of a jigsaw puzzle, all the pieces that were spread across the table suddenly swooping together to form a whole.

"Okay," her mother says brightly, "so if you don't have time to eat something with me then why don't I make you up a snack pack to share with Cara. If you guys are going to go nature hiking you'll need something to fortify you along the journey, don't you think?"

"Okay," Aimee says agreeably. "Thanks, Mom."

Her mother moves around the kitchen with practiced efficiency, gathering snacks and tucking them into a paper lunch bag. Chips, nuts, granola bars—not a thing that Aimee would ever let touch her lips.

It's okay, though, she thinks as her mother folds down the top of the bag and hands it to her with a tender smile. *I bet I know someone who'll eat them.*

When Aimee emerges from the scrappy woods behind the last row of condos out into the broad gray late afternoon, the fat girl (Meghan is her name) is waiting for her, planted by the end of the barn, a sky-blue blip against the beige-yellow cornstalks. As Aimee gets closer to her, she starts to have that mixed feeling that the fat girl (Meghan, *Meghan!*) always arouses in her. It's like putting her normal feelings into a blender and watching them spin and blur. Excitement, revulsion, curiosity, tenderness, fear, pity, shame, disgust . . . each feeling flashes cleanly through her and then gets sucked into the center of the emotion whirlpool. *This must be why no one's friends with her,* Aimee thinks. *How can you be friends with someone who makes you feel so many things at once just by looking at them?*

Meghan hovers, anchored at the barn's corner, hands shoved deep into the front pockets of her windbreaker, staring at Aimee unblinkingly as she approaches. Aimee tramps through the crunchy, ankle-high cornstalks feeling more watched than ever before in her life. When she makes it to about twenty feet away from the barn, Meghan lifts off her spot by the corner and comes toward Aimee. She smiles a little, just a very little.

"Hey," says Meghan.

"Hey," says Aimee.

"Follow me."

Aimee nods, smiles a very little back. Meghan turns and starts off across the cornfield, Aimee following as they head into the deep woods on the other side.

In the woods, as they tramp along a path that follows the bed of a little creek, Aimee can't take her eyes off the fat girl. She moves like a Macy's Thanksgiving Day Parade balloon, so heavy and so graceful at the same time. She's clearly been on this trail so many times that she could navigate it with her eyes closed—without even looking, she seems to know every branch to brush back, every log to clear, every rock to sidestep. She walks faster and faster the deeper they go into the woods; pretty soon Aimee's breaking into a jog every few steps to keep up.

The faster Aimee moves the floatier she feels—she thinks back, but she can't remember the last time she put something in her mouth. At her center Aimee feels her hunger harden into a steel rod, and her whole body starts to dissolve around it, vaporizing into a mist that spirals around that solid core. The smells of the forest intoxicate her: the tangy smell of pine needles, the smoky smell of decaying leaves, the tarnished-nickel smell of the water in the creek . . .

Ahead of her in the murky gray forest light the fat girl recedes and comes closer again, wavers in and out of focus. Suddenly Aimee has the feeling that she's fallen into a fairy tale, that she's following a huge, delicate supernatural creature—part beast, part sprite— back to its lair. Enchanted, she lets her eyes follow the fat girl's every movement, the way she reaches out to touch certain leaves and branches as if she's communicating with them or extracting magic oils from them. Although she's stumbling, barely able to keep up, it seems to Aimee from the depths of her trance that if she reaches out toward the creature or calls her name or disturbs her in any way the creature may spook and bolt, or turn around and cast a spell on Aimee, or vanish into a shimmer of air. . . .

After five minutes or fifty—Aimee has no idea—the fat girl turns back to look at her and holds aside a thick branch of pricker bush, gesturing for Aimee to pass by. They emerge into a grassy backyard: swingset with a canvas fort on top, mini trampoline, big blue two-story house, deck with a barbecue on it, garage to one side. Beyond the house Aimee can see other two-story houses a few wooded acres away. She rubs her eyes to sharpen her swimming vision.

The magical creature lives in a subdivision.

"You don't look so great," Meghan says to her. "Are you okay?"

"I've been sick," Aimee explains, trying to sound nonchalant but slurring her words.

"You need a drink of water or something? Or something to eat? Come on, come inside, I'll get you something to eat."

Aimee barely registers the walk up the wooden steps to the deck, the squeal of the plate-glass door as Meghan slides it open. The shift from cool outdoors to warm indoors as they enter. The distant coo of classical music, the enveloping smell of baking bread.

"Meegee!" From somewhere in the blurry room in front of them, the voice of a happy child.

"Oh—my goodness, who is this?" A warm voice, a surprised voice, a woman's voice.

"This is Aimee. Go ahead, Aimee, sit down." Meghan gives Aimee a little push, and Aimee feels herself folded into a chair.

She looks around her, makes out that the room they've walked into is an open-plan dining room/kitchen/den. The chair Aimee's sitting in is pulled out from a dining-room table heaped from end to end with random stuff—books, newspapers, half-finished puzzles, a vase with dried flowers in it, Transformers and G.I. Joes and X-Men, open pots of fingerpaint, a Monopoly board set up for the middle of a game.

"Drink this." Meghan reappears at Aimee's side with a red plastic cup full of water. Obediently, Aimee takes it and drinks. It tastes like cold crayons. Her vision begins to clear.

Across the table, behind the jumbled sea of stuff, Aimee sees a woman with an affectionate, chubby face and a single gray braid down her back sitting next to a small boy, maybe four years old, who's kneeling on a chair pounding his little fist into a lump of something sticky on the table.

"Meegee, we made play dough," the small boy tells Meghan.

"How awesome," Meghan says to him. Her face sweetens all over when she looks at him. "Aimee, this is my mom, Joanne. And this is my little brother Jesse."

"Hi," says Aimee.

"Welcome, Aimee," says Meghan's mom, Joanne. "Are you all right? You look a little faint."

"She's been sick, she just needs some water and maybe a snack," Meghan says before Aimee can open her mouth to explain. "Is there bread? Is it ready?"

"As a matter of fact, it wants to come out of the oven right about . . . now."

Joanne gets to her feet, revealing a short sturdy body in overalls and an apron smeared with streaks of paint, flour, glitter.

"Bread!" Jesse shrieks, whaling on his lump of play dough with both hands. "Me too bread, me too me too!"

As Joanne moves past Meghan into the kitchen area, she reaches up with both hands and squeezes Meghan's cheeks, smoothes her stringy bangs up off her forehead, and then kisses each of Meghan's round cheeks where her hands had been. There's a ritual quality to the series of gestures, like she's done them all a thousand times before in just that order.

"Beauty," she says, and beams at Meghan.

Meghan rolls her eyes. "Mom . . ."

As Joanne goes to deal with the bread, Meghan pulls out a chair next to Aimee's and sits down opposite her little brother.

"So buddy, what'd you do today?" she asks. Her voice in this house is open and calm and full of colors, so different from the narrow, tense voice Aimee's heard her use at school.

"Made play dough," Jesse answers fast. He reaches up to wipe his nose with the back of his hand and leaves a smear of play dough across the middle of his face. Meghan doesn't mention it.

"And what else?"

"Went to see the miniature donkeys."

"This guy down the street has a little field with these two miniature donkeys." Meghan fills Aimee in. "Jesse likes to go look at them and feed them lumps of sugar. What're their names, buddy?"

"Fred and Ginger," Jesse says, fast again, like Meghan's testing him to see how quickly he can answer. Then he turns to Aimee and addresses her seriously: "What's the rule?"

"Um, I don't know what you mean," Aimee says.

"No, what's the *rule* with Fred and Ginger?" Jesse demands impatiently. "Hands flat, hands flat, that's the rule!"

"You have to keep your hand flat while you're feeding the donkeys the lumps of sugar or they might bite you a little," Meghan explains.

"Oh . . ."

"See?" Jesse holds his doughy hands up in a gesture of total obviousness, like Aimee is being ridiculously obtuse.

"Bread, bread, bread," Joanne announces as she brings a big plate of thickly cut slices of white bread down into the center of the cluttered table. The plate balances, slanted, half on and half off a collapsing stack of old *National Geographic* magazines, but to Aimee it's a beautiful thing to behold—the bread is so freshly baked that it's steaming, and the smell that comes off it is like an embrace, as warm and comforting as flannel bedclothes or a freshly washed towel after a bath.

"Everyone help themselves," Joanne urges, and Meghan and Jesse both reach over and grab slices of bread off the serving plate. Aimee watches Meghan tear into her piece with her teeth, feels something she hasn't felt in a long time: her mouth watering.

Tentatively, Aimee reaches out to touch one of the pieces of bread, just to see what will happen. She hasn't made any physical contact with an actual piece of bread in months, maybe even a year—the reaction could be major. She lets her fingertips just brush the surface of the last piece of bread on the plate. It's soft and inviting; she listens for the sizzle but hears nothing. Now she puts her whole hand down on the slice, feels its warmth spreading across her palm and rushing up her arm. She's about to start massaging the piece of bread a little, to make absolutely sure it's not going to trigger a reaction, when she realizes that all three other people in the room have stopped what they were doing and are watching her curiously.

"What are you doing?" Jesse asks.

"Um . . ."

"Go ahead, Aimee," Joanne says encouragingly. "Try it. I think you'll like it."

Fighting back a wave of fear, Aimee brings the warm piece of bread to her mouth, bites off a tiny piece. And chews.

She expects sizzle, she expects nausea, she expects oblivion. But what she gets is flavor. Wheaty, yeasty, warm. The tiny bite of bread fills Aimee's mouth with the flavor of safety, and of joy.

"It's good," she says, her voice small. She's afraid if she says anything more she might cry.

Joanne smiles big. "I knew it," she grins. "Nobody doesn't like my bread." She comes around to sit back down beside Jesse, puts her hand on the back of his neck in a casual gesture of adoration. "So you girls want to do some play-dough sculpting with us? We're going to make animals and robots, right Jess?"

"That's okay," Meghan says hurriedly. "Actually Aimee came over 'cause we're working on this project. We'll just take some bread up to my room."

Meghan's room is nothing like Aimee would have imagined, if she had ever bothered to imagine it. But it's exactly like the rest of her cluttered house. Her room is like the back room of a cheap antique shop—every single surface is covered with stuff, seemingly from every phase of a person's life, from a My Little Pony collection displayed on one shelf to a full set of leather-bound supermarket encyclopedias lined up on another, from heaps of dirty clothes to a chemistry set to a pile of teddy bears in one corner, from stacks of chunky paperback novels to what looks like a bug-catching kit spread out on the floor by the bed. Every single inch of wall space is covered with pictures of actors torn from magazines or posters, posters overlapping posters, of everything from Maroon 5 to maps of the world to pictures of Saturn and its rings. On the wall by the head of the unmade bed is a signed, framed photograph of Hillary Clinton.

Meghan settles herself on the floor among the piles of stuff, leans back against her bed, and rests her crossed arms on the hump of her belly.

"Your mom's nice," Aimee offers, looking around her for a bare spot of floor to sit on. Meghan reaches out and clears a space in the debris with a swipe of her arm, shoving a short stack of *Teen People* magazines and two naked Barbies and a tangle of pink-and-white ankle socks under her bed.

"Yeah," Meghan agrees. "She's super nice. She doesn't see anything she doesn't want to see. That keeps her happy."

Aimee notices a shadow slip through Meghan's eyes as she says this, a brief moment of cloud cover.

"What do you mean?" Aimee asks. Meghan shakes her head.

"Whatever," she says, shaking her head to dismiss the whole topic. "The point of us being here isn't my mom, it's Cara. She stole your poem, and now you want revenge."

"Uh, no," Aimee says, startled. "I never said anything about revenge. I just want my poem back."

"Okay. Okay." Meghan seems to think this over.

Aimee is mesmerized by the bulge of Meghan's neck, the expanse of her chest under her T-shirt, her great sloping belly. She steals quick looks at Meghan's astonishing body, trying not to lapse into stares no matter how much she wants to consume her with her eyes.

"You might end up accidentally getting revenge on her," Meghan says thoughtfully, "if you steal something from her. I mean, stealing is not a very nice thing to do. Revenge might be unavoidable, I don't know."

A curious look, calm but rippling with energy, passes over Meghan when she says the word *revenge*, as if her face is the surface of a glassy lake full of dark creatures thrashing around in its depths.

"Okay," Aimee offers tentatively. "If it's unavoidable, I guess."

"What does she get for winning this competition?"

"Um, well first of all, she gets the poem read aloud during morning announcements on Monday."

Meghan smiles faintly. "Interesting," she murmurs.

"And then the poem gets sent to Washington, D.C., to be judged by famous writers and—you know what, it doesn't even matter what she gets, I don't care about that. I just want my poem back, that's all I care about."

"Okay, we're gonna steal it back. If it's gonna be read during announcements on Monday then it'll be in a manila folder in the top left-hand drawer of Ms. Champoux's desk by one o'clock tomorrow."

"How do you know that?"

Meghan shrugs her shadow shrug, so small it's more like a change in her attitude than in her physical position.

"The secretaries have a routine. Ms. Deckel finishes putting together the next day's announcements by the end of D period. Then Ms. Frattarola proofreads them by the end of E period. Then Ms. Champoux puts them in the folder in her desk by the end of F period. I'll swing by the office during G period tomorrow and lift it. Easy."

"Can you do that?"

"It's just bio, no big deal. Ms. Snell is wicked brain damaged from years of handling the formaldehyded frogs with no gloves. She's delirious half the time. She barely notices me when I *am* there."

"No, yeah, but I mean, can you steal something out of a desk right in the middle of the front office? During school?"

"Can I steal from Ms. *Champoux*?" Meghan waves the question away. "Please. Like candy from a baby. I've lifted passes from her desk a billion times."

"Passes?"

As Meghan's secret life of crime begins to take shape in Aimee's eyes she feels a flash of fearful respect for the girl sitting almost motionless across from her.

"Blank passes," Meghan says simply. "For freedom of movement."

"Freedom of movement," Aimee echoes.

"The swiping part's totally easy. What's hard is figuring out what to switch it with."

"Well, why do we have to switch it with anything?" Aimee asks.

"Because . . ." Meghan looks up at the ceiling, thinking. Aimee follows her gaze and is surprised to see a poster of a family of meerkats tacked up there. "Because it's an opportunity, I guess. This thing is going to be read out loud to the whole school, with Cara's name attached to it. Can you imagine what that could do for us?"

"But I, I don't want it to *do* anything for us, I just don't want people to think my poem is hers."

"Okay, I get it. You're a nice person." Meghan peers at Aimee intently and Aimee gets that creepy ticklish feeling—the same feeling she got every time she caught Meghan staring at her from across a parking lot or hallway or room—as if Meghan's gaze is weirdly sucking something out of her and glazing her with a protective coating at the same time. "But aren't you even a *little* mad at her?" Meghan leans forward a little and looks so deeply at Aimee that Aimee has to look away. "She stole your private thoughts, doesn't that piss you off? You trusted her, and you opened up to her, and she totally betrayed you. Doesn't she deserve to be punished a little?"

"Maybe," Aimee says reluctantly.

"Definitely, I think. And see, here's what we can do—it'll be so simple. You can write a new poem and sign Cara's name to it, and during G period tomorrow when I swipe her stolen poem I'll just replace it with the decoy one you wrote. Then Ms. Champoux will read the decoy on Monday morning, and everyone will think Cara wrote it. There won't be anything she can do."

Aimee squirms uncomfortably. "I don't know," she says. "What should I write for the decoy? Maybe something, like, with a really awkward meter or something, so people think she doesn't understand iambic pentameter?"

But Meghan is completely lost in a reverie, Aimee sees. Her eyes are open but all they're seeing is what she's imagining—they flicker with delight at the scene she sees playing out in her mind. After a moment she comes back down to earth, registers Aimee's presence in the room, and smiles a deliciously mischievous smile.

"I've got it," she says, hushed. "I know what the decoy has to be about. Get a pen. Do you have paper? I'll get you some paper. You need to take notes." As Aimee reaches into her satchel for a pen, Meghan rummages under her bed, feeling around with her hand until she pulls out—improbably—a crisp brand-new legal pad, which she shoves abruptly in Aimee's direction. "Now I'm going to tell you a story," Meghan says, "and your job is to turn it into a poem that sounds like it's from Cara's point of view."

"I'm ready." Aimee feels her heart beating fast, feels herself caught up suddenly in the excitement of the project.

"Okay," Meghan says, and closes her eyes. "Picture a shed, in a field of tall grass behind an old house on Sunset Avenue. . . ."

• 17 •

G period. Meghan is on her mission to the office, but something major is going down. As she approaches the office door she sees that Ms. Champoux is blocking it from the inside, her back pressed against it to keep people out. Inside, Meghan sees Dr. Dempsey arguing with Mr. Handsley. Clearly their fight has spilled out of the principal's office into the main office. Meghan's desperate to hear the content of what's going on—she scuttles around the corner and down the hall a few feet to the interoffice mail room, which has an access door at the back of it leading into the hall with Dr. Dempsey's office. Luckily that door is unguarded, and she eases through it and lodges in this back hall, watching from the shadows as the scene unfolds in the outer office.

"This student claims that you manhandled him—"

"Manhandled!" Mr. Handsley cries, aghast. "*Manhandled*, that is a ridiculous allegation! I have never *manhandled* a student in my thirty-eight years of teaching, nor do I intend to *manhandle* a single student in however many years I may have left. That is a preposterous allegation. I barely touched the boy."

"But you did touch him."

A pause. Meghan feels her heart sink. *No, Mr. Handsley,* she thinks, *say no!*

Mr. Handsley speaks carefully. "I made light physical contact with Mr. Bartlett's solar plexus to encourage him to utilize his abdominal muscles to project his voice into the auditorium."

"You touched his stomach?"

"I lightly tapped . . . in the middle of a group of . . . in a roomful of . . . I was coaching him through a performance!"

"The parents are real unhappy about this, Joe. And Rich is behind them."

"I'm stunned to hear it," Mr. Handsley says drily.

"He's pushing for disciplinary action."

"Against *me*?" Once again Mr. Handsley gasps. "You're telling me that man never touches his athletes when he's coaching them? He never once makes physical contact?"

"What Rich does when he coaches isn't the issue here. The issue here is what happened in that auditorium."

Another pause. Meghan imagines Mr. Handsley slumping down in his vinyl chair.

"This is harassment," Mr. Handsley says quietly.

"Yes, that's the charge the Bartletts are going to bring."

"No, of *me*! This is harassment of me! I gave thirty-eight years of my life to this school and I've labored to keep our graduates from sinking ever deeper into the mire of unpreparedness every year, and now this yahoo is trying to badger me out of my job so you can install some shrinking violet in my place who will hand out gentlemen's Cs to every one of his so-called athletes."

"There's no conspiracy here, Joe, and I think you know it. Between you and Rich I don't know which of you is more paranoid."

"That man has been trying to get me fired since the day he arrived!"

"Rich Cox doesn't call the shots around here, I do."

"Then rein him in! Don't let him do this to me!"

"I'm afraid I'm with Rich on this one, Joe. I have to put the welfare of the student body first."

Now there's the kind of stunned silence that follows a slap. When Mr. Handsley speaks again his voice sounds broken.

"If you think I'm a threat to the student body . . . if that's the position of the administration of this school, then I will not stay here another minute."

"Now, Joe—"

"I will not remain in the employ of an administration that sees me that way."

"Joe—"

"I tender my resignation, effective immediately."

"Joe, will you please be reasonable here?"

Meghan hears Mr. Handsley storming toward her hiding place and flattens herself as quickly as she can behind the nearest filing cabinet. When Mr. Handsley strides past her on his way out the door, he comes so close she can smell his dandruff shampoo.

• • •

After school, Music Practice Room D. Aimee looks up expectantly when Meghan tugs open the door.

Aimee is sitting cross-legged on the filthy carpet, her back pressed against the graffiti-covered, pockmarked wall. Meghan almost never has the fluorescents on when she's in here, and as well as she feels like she should know this place, she's noticing some details as she looks around that she never saw before. Once, long ago before the advent of Ritalin and Adderall, this practice room was used as a prison cell for kids with "behavior problems." The walls bear witness to this abandoned purpose—Meghan can't believe, as she looks around at them now, that she never noticed before how they scream out against injustice on all four sides: FIGHT BACK, says the wall above the piano in jagged Sharpie letters; RAGE AGAINST THE MACHINE, the wall by the door urges in letters carved a half an inch deep into the crumbling drywall. SUCK ME DEMPSEY, commands the wall above the garbage can. Aimee sits in the middle of this silent riot, stick legs crossed in their black fishnets, more a reed in the river than a Buddha, but still beatific.

"So? Did you get it?" Aimee asks, hopeful.

"I tried, but there was a big thing going on in the office during G period—I couldn't get to the desk. I could try to lift it now but I just passed the office and Ms. Champoux is in there alone—I just don't see how I can do it if she's the only one in there. I need at least a few seconds of distraction."

"What about me? I can be very distracting," Aimee offers.

"I don't know . . . I don't think that's such a good idea. The office is a really sensitive place."

"Well can you wait and go do it after she leaves?"

"No." Meghan shakes her head. "She's always the last out on Fridays, and she locks the place down when she goes. They've got grades in there and disciplinary files—they shut the main office up like a bank vault."

"Well we have to do this now," Aimee says, her voice rising. "This is our last chance before Monday morning. I think you should let me help you. I might be more useful than you think."

Meghan deliberates a beat, then nods.

"Okay," she says.

At the door to the office Meghan leans down to speak low into Aimee's ear.

"Ask her about the new in-school suspension rules," she whispers.

"Ask her what about them?"

"Ask her if she thinks they're justified under juvenile criminal law. She has a lot of opinions about that."

"But why would I walk into the office after school and ask her about juvenile criminal law?"

"Tell her you're working on an article for the school paper and you heard she was an informed source about the issue of in-school suspensions. She's going to go for it, I promise. Then I'll come around and make the trade in her announcements folder while she's not looking."

"She'll see you, she'll totally see you!"

Around the edge of this Meghan hears the unspoken implication: *How can she not see you?*

"She won't see me," Meghan says. "I promise. I've been right under her nose a million times and she never, ever sees me. Trust me."

Aimee looks dubious, but when they walk through the door Ms. Champoux looks up, makes eye contact with Aimee only, and says, "Yes? What can I do you for?"

Meghan melts aside.

"Um, yeah, I'm writing a thing for the . . ." Meghan freezes as Aimee searches her mind for the name of the student paper. *Valley Voice,* Meghan transmits to Aimee in violent ESP. *Valley Voice, Valley Voice!* ". . . um, school paper? About the new in-school suspension laws?"

"Dr. Dempsey's gone for the day," Ms. Champoux drones, thoroughly bored.

"Um, no, I wanted to ask *you* some questions," Aimee persists, rigging her face with a polite smile.

"Me?" Ms. Champoux says warily. "Why me? What do I have anything to do with the new rules?"

"I just heard that you're a highly informed source about, um, the way the new rules, um, relate to juvenile criminal law? And so um, do you have any thoughts on that?"

Out of the corner of her eye, as she glides around the side of the reception counter and moves into the center of the office, Meghan registers Ms. Champoux's transformation from scowling attack dog to flattered interviewee. Her whole face warms and softens. Even her perm seems to relax.

"Well as a matter of fact I do. I don't know who told you but as a matter of fact I do have some thoughts on that."

Ms. Champoux leans toward Aimee, propping her elbows up on the reception desk and making herself comfortable—Meghan is a little shocked to see her kick off one scuffed high-heeled shoe and rub her pantyhosed foot on the opposite calf as she begins to talk.

"Well first of all, public school and juvenile detention—they're not as far apart as you might think."

Out of her satchel, Aimee produces a notebook and a pen and begins to take notes as Ms. Champoux expounds on the new cruel and unusual punishments the regional superintendent has devised for out-of-control students.

As she draws open Ms. Champoux's desk drawer, the one where she keeps the master calendar and the morning announcements folder, the one that clicks and squeaks when it's two-thirds of the way open, Meghan has a funny sensation. She feels like she's at once liquid and solid, visible and invisible—she made it all the way over here without making herself disappear. She's opening one of the best-guarded vaults of secrets in the entire school right here in broad daylight, and she's not even made of mist, and still no one is watching her.

"Oh, really?" Aimee says encouragingly from the other side of the counter.

"Oh, yes!" Ms. Champoux enthuses, nodding vigorously. They're having a real conversation. Ms. Champoux could clearly go on about this topic for hours. Meghan feels like she has all the time in the world.

She finesses the drawer over the telltale click and squeak with a practiced hitch of her wrist. The announcements folder is on the top of the pile inside, beat up and very familiar. She slips her finger under the cover to find the purloined poem on the very top of the stack of papers to be read on Monday morning. Too easy, all too easy. She makes the switch smoothly, hands crossing and poems fluttering, like a white-gloved magician conjuring a rabbit from a hat. Close folder, shut drawer, glide back toward Aimee and the escape hatch of the office door.

"But so you're saying it's sort of a violation of a kid's human rights to be incarcerated during the day with nothing to do?" Aimee seems to be as deeply involved in her conversation with Ms. Champoux as Ms. Champoux is.

"It sure enough would be, if this weren't a school. But in a school, now, you can get away with all kinds of things that can't happen in the real world. You get what I mean?"

Meghan drifts behind Aimee toward the front door of the office, hoping to catch her attention without having to speak to her.

"Um, this is so interesting," Aimee says to Ms. Champoux, "but I have to go, I have to . . . catch the late bus. Can I come back and talk to you more about this on Monday?"

"You surely can," Ms. Champoux says, smiling as radiantly as a newly crowned beauty queen. "It's refreshing to have a student take an interest in the nuts and bolts of disciplinary reform. About time. And tell your classmates. This affects all of you, you know."

"She is so *weird*, that woman," Aimee says admiringly, leaning her back against the wall outside the office door and scribbling furiously in her notebook.

"What are you doing?"

"I just want to make a couple notes before I forget what I saw. I think I might want to write a poem about Ms. Champoux."

"Speaking of . . ."

Aimee looks up from the page and Meghan offers her the twice-stolen poem. Aimee's face breaks into a joyful smile and she snatches the poem from Meghan's hand.

"You did it! And she didn't even notice!"

"No one ever does," says Meghan proudly. "Okay, so I was thinking one last thing: just to be double-triple sure about this, I want to go check the *Photon* box and make sure there's not, like, a spare copy floating around in there. Just on the off chance something goes wrong, or in case after it gets read Cara's upset and goes looking for evidence. We just want to cover our tracks."

"Smart," says Aimee, "but I'm not going in there. Cara could be in that office doing editorial stuff, and I'm not going anyplace she might be."

"That's cool," says Meghan. "I can handle it. It's just a quick sweep."

"It'd be in the *Photon* box on Mr. Handsley's desk, the one by the—"

"Please," Meghan interrupts. "I know exactly what I'm doing."

Meghan lets herself into the English office as quietly as possible. She scans the room, but it appears to be empty. Late afternoon light, rich as butterscotch pudding, streams in through the ancient venetian blinds. Meghan makes her way to Mr. Handsley's desk and begins

rummaging through the stacks of papers on it, searching for the page
with the long, thin poem on it.

"Looking for something?"

Meghan freezes mid-rifle.

Across the room, Mr. Handsley rises from where he has been
crouched down in front of a filing cabinet, out of sight.

"Please don't tell me Meghan Ball, of all people, is trying to cheat.
I don't believe my battered heart could withstand the impact of that
one. If Meghan Ball is trying to cheat, my heart may just break right
here in my chest."

Meghan's barely breathing. She shakes her head, mute.

Mr. Handsley nudges the bottom drawer of the filing cabinet
closed with his toe, and Meghan notices that all around him on the
floor are open cardboard boxes half full of papers and files. He's
already packing up his stuff.

"Well?" Mr. Handsley slips his hands into the pockets of his cor-
duroy slacks and strolls toward Meghan casually, as if he's got all the
time in the world to cross the room. "Surely *that's* not what you're
after." He gestures with a jerk of his white-bearded chin at the paper
in Meghan's hands, the one she happened to be holding when he
called her out. Meghan looks down at it; it's the master sheet for the
Julius Caesar vocabulary quiz from two weeks ago, the one she got
a 93 on. Countenance=face. Bootless=useless. "You got a ninety-
three on that, didn't you?" Mr. Handsley remarks amiably. "You only
missed 'countenance' and 'bootless,' so I can't imagine why you'd
want to look it over again. May I?"

Mr. Handsley has reached the desk now, and he leans across it, thumb and forefinger poised, and plucks the quiz from Meghan's hands, lays it back down on the desk and pats it tidily. Meghan's palms have gone sweaty, and she's panting tiny pants, like a bunny cornered by a wolf. In all the years she's been watching, listening, looking, she's never had the feeling of getting caught before.

"Have a seat, please."

Meghan starts to lower herself into the desk chair behind her, but Mr. Handsley cries out, "Not in *my* chair, please, here, here, the *victim's* chair." He points to a spindly metal folding chair set up against the wall by his desk, clearly the place he makes students sit when they come here to conference, or cry, or confess their sins against Shakespeare. "*I'll* assume the throne, thank you very much."

Meghan maneuvers out of the narrow space between Mr. Handsley's desk and the wall and sits gingerly on the folding chair; she can feel it mustering all its pitiful strength to hold her up as she gradually trusts her full weight to it. Mr. Handsley settles himself somewhat grandly in his squeaky desk chair, crossing his legs, knitting his hands together behind his head, and leaning back as if he means to sunbathe beneath the fluorescents.

"So, what *were* you looking for?"

Meghan shrugs a slight shrug and stares down at the floor. Such ugly tiles—terminally ill gray with little flecks of red and blue scattered across them—and somebody actually made them like this *on purpose.* It strikes Meghan now, as she tries with all her might to absent herself from this confrontation she's having, that every ugly thing in this school was intentionally designed by someone to look and function as it does. Chairs intentionally made small and uncom-

fortable, tiles intentionally made butt ugly—the conspiracy of depri-
vation and humiliation that is high school extending all the way to
the manufacturers of floor tiles and chairs—

"Handsley to Meghan Ball—come in, Ball." Mr. Handsley broad-
casts into Meghan's vacant reverie, his hands cupped around his
mouth for effect. Reluctantly, Meghan lifts her eyes to his face.
"Your purpose in rummaging through my things?" he prompts, but
Meghan can only shrug apologetically and look down again. Mr.
Handsley sighs.

"Look," he begins, undoing his kicked-back position and sitting
up to face her squarely, "there's something I've been wanting to say
to you for some time, and since it looks like I might not be around
here much longer I'm just going to come out and say it. All right?"
Meghan nods. "I get kind of a strong feeling off you, Meghan Ball,
that you think nobody else in the world can see you. You sit in the
corner and you never say boo and you generally keep the lowest
profile of any student I've ever taught—and my dear, at this point
in my career I've taught *thousands*. In a certain way I admire your
disappearing act. It's hard work not being noticed, and I speak from
experience. I spent years, *decades*, killing myself trying not to be
seen."

"*You?*" Meghan asks in frank disbelief.

Mr. Handsley smiles devilishly.

"Yes, me, and I'll take your obvious shock as a compliment,
because that part of my life is long over. I have no interest in keeping
silent or blending in anymore. But I remember all too well what it
felt like to be invisible—I used to imagine that I was holding up a big

one-way mirror, you know, that I could look through to see everyone else but that no one could look through to see me. Does that sound familiar?"

Meghan shrugs noncommittally.

"Well, after a while you realize that the big mirror you think you're hiding behind is really just a clear pane of glass, and people have been seeing right through it all along. Like me. I see you. Would you like me to tell you what I see?"

Meghan gives Mr. Handsley a pained look: *Not really.*

"Great, I'll take your silence as a yes, which by the way is what everyone else will do, too. As long as you never open your mouth and tell other people how to treat you, they're going to treat you however they please, maybe even quite badly, and they'll take your silence as permission to do so. Don't let that happen, you mustn't let that happen to you!"

To Meghan's surprise, Mr. Handsley flushes bright pink and starts to tremble a little, as if he's struggling to control himself.

"When I look at you, Ms. Ball, what I see is a lovely young woman who is bright and strong and sensitive, and so observant I can actually observe you observing sometimes."

Meghan feels stripped bare by this revelation; impulsively she moves to retract herself, pull herself in.

"I see how closely you pay attention to everything. I bet you know everything about everybody, don't you. Tell me something I don't know about . . ." He looks up at the ceiling, as if running through a mental class roster. "Rebecca Trainer."

Without missing a beat Meghan says, "Her mom was Miss Massachusetts twenty years ago, but she told Becky that her proportions and her teeth are wrong for pageants and she'll never get anywhere off of her looks."

Mr. Handsley barks a short, rueful laugh.

"Interesting," he says. "Enlightening, actually. I bet you can do that with every kid in this school, can't you."

Meghan shrugs. "Most of them."

"So you take all this stuff in but you never put anything out. I'm telling you, that's no way to live. If you were more like Jonah I wouldn't worry so much about you."

"Jonah *Boyd*?"

"I'm not saying you'd want to be like him in every way, I'm just saying that the boy has moxie, he's got a mouth on him. You've seen him, he never misses a chance to stand up for himself."

"Because he's an idiot," Meghan says, low.

"Now, see, I disagree. He employs a different strategy than you do, that's all."

"He doesn't even hear what people say about him half the time."

"That's exactly right, and is that such a bad thing? Has he been hurt by one nasty thing that someone else has said to him when he wasn't paying attention?"

"No, but . . ." Meghan tries desperately to summon the words to describe the humiliation, rage, and disgust she feels on behalf of Jonah every time someone says something about him that he cheerfully doesn't acknowledge.

"And when he talks back to his enemies, when he yells back right in young J-Bar's face, what happens? Is he injured? Is he even threatened?"

"They'd kill me," Meghan whispers, barely audible.

"I know it feels that way, but you'd be surprised how well people respond when you stand up to them."

"Like how you stood up to Dr. Dempsey about J-Bar?" She doesn't mean for it to come out as mean-sounding as it does.

Mr. Handsley's expression skips a beat. He takes a breath, smoothes over the hairline fracture in his composure. When he speaks, he speaks sharply.

"What do you know about that?"

Meghan shakes her head vigorously, trying to take it back: *Nothing.*

Mr. Handsley seems like he's about to gear up for one of his rants. Meghan braces herself. "Look," he begins bluntly, but then stops, seems to wilt back against his chair. He exhales a measured breath. "I feel as if have been standing up to people for a very long time," he says thoughtfully, "and this afternoon, quite all of a sudden, I came to the end of my line. If young people want to play Wiffle ball or Masters of Doom or Internet poker instead of performing the works of the greatest writer in the history of the English language, who am I to tell them they shouldn't? I've done what I can with young J-Bar and his cohort. I've done what I can with you."

Mr. Handsley gives Meghan a look of such ragged weariness that it embarrasses her—it's a private look, a face so unguarded that it doesn't belong in a high-school English office. Flustered, Meghan gets to her feet and makes for the door.

"Ms. Ball," Mr. Handsley calls out behind her.

Meghan stops, turns halfway around. The sight of Mr. Handsley slumped in his throne, surrounded by boxes overflowing with his belongings, hits her hard. He looks old; he looks unhooked from his energy source.

"You never said what you were looking for on my desk."

"It doesn't matter," Meghan says quietly.

He nods and seems to be waiting for her to go, but she doesn't move. She can't walk away without saying something more, something final, to him. She wants to tell him that she loves *Julius Caesar*, that his class is the only one she's never walked out of. She wants to tell him that she loves him for never calling on her when she didn't want to talk, and for never making her read out loud when they went around the room, and for letting her work the curtain backstage instead of exposing her to public ridicule on stage in a giant bedsheet.

"Then is there something else I can help you with?"

"I wish you wouldn't leave," Meghan mumbles self-consciously.

Mr. Handsley's face softens. He looks away from Meghan for a moment, puts his hand to his chest and pats it lightly, as if checking to make sure his heart is there, the way a man pats his pocket to check for his wallet.

"Truly, dear heart," he says after a moment, looking not at Meghan but down at his desk, "I wish I didn't have to go."

In Music Practice Room D, Aimee is waiting.

"Did you find another copy?" she asks eagerly.

Meghan shakes her head.

"Did you bump into anyone in the office?"

Again Meghan shakes her head.

"Okay, so now what do we do?"

"Now," Meghan says calmly, "we wait."

• 18 •

Monday.

First real cold morning of fall. Silvery coating of frost over the whole town, the whole school. Kids still in their skimpy early fall clothes, chattering on their hurried way between the buses and the front doors. The drop-off road billowing with smoky bus exhaust and the frozen breath of teenagers.

Meghan is shivering inside her windbreaker on her bench, on the lookout for Bus 12. She imagines standing up as Aimee gets off the bus, imagines walking over to her, imagines Aimee lighting up with a smile when she sees Meghan. Imagines them walking through the front door together, lingering and giggling until the second bell rings and they have to tear themselves away from each other to go to their separate homerooms to wait out the last few moments before the Event.

But as Bus 12 rounds the corner of the school and rumbles toward

Meghan, she rapidly cycles through another vision of the morning: awkward meeting out front, uncomfortable silence walking through the doors, strain of small talk in the hall—nothing to say—split into separate homerooms, wait out the last few moments before . . . nothing happens. What if something has gone horribly wrong? What if over the weekend someone has intercepted their interception? What if the decoy is still there but Ms. Champoux reads it wrong, or what if she reads it right and nobody cares, nobody even notices the difference or gets the reference? What if the whole thing is a total anticlimax and Aimee thinks she's stupid and never speaks to her again?

Bus 12 squeals and gasps to a stop not twenty yards away from Meghan and she sees the unmistakable silhouette inside: floppy hat, sharp shoulders, moving down the aisle. Meghan panics, gets to her feet, gathers her backpack and presses it clumsily to her gut, and hustles as fast as she can in the direction of the front door, away from Aimee Zorn.

Aimee peers out the window of Bus 12 just in time to see the unmistakable blue windbreaker slip inside the front door of the school. Aimee's plan to find Meghan and set up a time to meet and debrief after morning announcements goes up in smoke as she watches Meghan trundle away.

Inside, in homeroom, Aimee can hardly sit still. The desk is the only thing holding her down as she stares up at the clock, barely noticing the room fill up with kids all around her, willing the minute hand to leap forward from 7:47 to 7:52. 7:48 to 7:52. 7:49 to 7:52.

The rest of the world burns away as Aimee focuses her entire being on the sleeping/leaping minute hand of the clock.

7:52.

The familiar burst of static.

"Good morning students faculty and staff. It is my pleasure to welcome you. To Monday morning."

"Settle down now, I said settle *down* now, or I'll write out one-way tickets to the new in-school suspension for every single one of you. Make your day, right, people? You want me to make your day?"

Mr. Cox looks bloated and beat up this morning, like he spent the night under a bridge. His whole pink head is a size larger than usual but his eyes look smaller—they seem sunken into the dough of his face like raisins pressed into a cinnamon roll.

"I got one blank pass for each one of you people and a list of your G.D. names right here, I'll just transfer 'em right over. Roster, pass. Roster, pass."

Mr. Cox demonstrates how he'll make their day, holding up a sample blank pass and the attendance list for homeroom C23 and pointing back and forth from one to the other. But the room has an irrepressible buoyancy to it this morning—the kids are giddy and silly and can't be intimidated. Even J-Bar's in a rare goofy mood, ignoring Mr. Cox and making teasing jokes across the aisle to Shane and Monica Balan. Meghan floats on the warm current of the class's collective happiness—she knows, even though they don't, what they're really waiting for.

"This morning we have eh special meditation written by eh

member of thee student body of Valley Regional High who is thee winner of thee annual Autumn Poetry Competition."

Meghan's pulse begins to flutter in her neck.

"We are very proud to read her winning poem alongside thee poems by published poets we have been reading. Dr. Dempsey does ask that you please observe thee silent thirty-second meditation period after thee reading as usual."

Is it Meghan's imagination, or is Ms. Champoux speaking in almost complete sentences this morning?

"'Shed Love,' by Cara Roy," Ms. Champoux intones.

> *"The golden basketball boy*
> *comes to me when he is sad because*
> *he knows I am the only one who can give him comfort."*

It seems to Aimee that Ms. Champoux has undergone some kind of radical speech therapy over the weekend. Her voice is clear and calm, every one of her consonants is crisply articulated, and the nasal buzz that made her sound like a Muppet with a head cold has miraculously fallen away from her tone.

She sounds a little . . . happy?

> *"Everyone thinks the golden basketball boy*
> *feels no pain*
> *everyone thinks his blond hair and captain's jersey*
> *protect him from sorrow.*
> *But no one knows like I do*

how grief lives in his heart,
curled up there like a soft, abandoned puppy."

C23 is already starting to bubble with curiosity, like a pot just starting to simmer on the burner.

"The golden basketball boy comes to me when he is sad," Ms. Champoux reads,

"because he knows I will never tell
how he cries when he misses an easy layup
how he misses his mom when he goes away to camp
how his puppy means more to him than anything.
I meet him here in the shed
behind the old abandoned house
every afternoon and take his golden head in my lap
and show him what it means to love.
He may be number 17 on the team
but he is number 1 in my heart."

A couple of stifled gasps from the kids in homeroom. Kaitlyn Carmigan claps her hand over her mouth to keep from bursting out laughing. Kids are turning in their seats to look at J-Bar, who's sinking slowly down in his. The big white number 17 on the back of his letterman jacket is half-concealed now by the back of his chair.

"What I know now about golden basketball boys
is that they only look tough on the outside.
On the inside they are as soft as caramels

soft as kisses
soft as babies.
I am the only one J-Bar has ever truly loved"

At the name "J-Bar" Mr. Cox looks up at the PA speaker, shocked—

"and I will treasure that love until the day I die.
I will keep his painful secrets as I keep my own.
I will never let his golden light go
out."

A pause. Total silence. The first actually silent silent meditation period since the first day of school.

Nobody seems to have a clue what to do. Mr. Cox turns to J-Bar with an open question on his face. All the kids hang in suspended animation, unsure whether to burst out laughing or save their own butts by keeping quiet. Even Ms. Champoux's PA silence seems confused.

Meghan closes her eyes and rides the silence, feels the energy of J-Bar's humiliation stretching out in all directions around her, flowing from the epicenter—C23—to the four corners of the Earth, washing over everyone in the world.

Then, as if Meghan had scripted it herself, Ms. Champoux comes back over the PA to make sure no one missed it. "*Ahem.* That was 'Shed Love,' thee winner of thee Valley Regional Autumn Poetry Competition. By *Cara Roy.*"

"What in the H?" Mr. Cox demands from the front of the

room. "Bartlett, is that you? Is she talking about you?"

J-Bar's face is raspberry red, boiling against the starchy yellow of his hair. Meghan can practically see the heat of his body rippling the air around him.

The whole homeroom begins to laugh, but Meghan barely hears it—the burning of J-Bar is playing out like a silent, slow-motion film across the room from her. He's trembling now, the sweat on his temples practically steaming off him in wisps.

"Stud," says Shane, snarky-funny. He whacks J-Bar hard on the back, flat between his shoulder blades, and suddenly Shane's head is snapping back, recoiling from the impact of J-Bar's fist, which has shot out to punch him so fast Meghan missed the movement. Shane's face registers an instant of shock, a split-second of hurt, before he's on his feet whaling on J-Bar, who clatters out of his chair to beat on him for real.

Everybody scatters to the sides of the room, hooting and yelling like Romans at the Colosseum as the varsity gladiators explode down the center aisle, toppling desks, sending books and binders skittering across the floor, grappling, grunting, trying to tear each other's throats out.

J-Bar looks like a wild animal who's escaped from his cage, as if he's been pent up for years, just waiting to unleash this savage part of himself into the world.

"Hey hey *hey*!" Mr. Cox yells, but he's barely audible above the din of the spectators, Ms. Champoux mooing her way through the rest of the announcements, and the animal growls of J-Bar and Shane. "Break it up, gentlemen, I said break it up!"

Mr. Cox heaves his way out from behind his desk, shoves both meaty hands into the blur of basketball captains and begins to pry them apart, grunting with the effort.

It's mayhem. Nobody's watching her. Delirious with success, Meghan melts from the room.

Aimee waits until the bell rings, grinding the gears of the school forward into A period, then hurries as fast as she can away from her first class toward Music Practice Room D.

As she rounds the corner into the art hall, she sees Meghan already lodged in the corner at the far end, peering with exquisite focus through the window of the practice room. Meghan looks up as Aimee comes skidding into the hall and puts one finger to her lips in warning, beckons her forward slightly with the other hand.

When Aimee comes close enough to see through the window she realizes what's keeping Meghan outside: J-Bar is in there, screaming at someone. The room is so thickly paneled, so insulated against sound leakage that it's impossible to make out what he's saying as he yells—still it's clear that he's screaming abuse, his arms flailing in the air around him. He paces to one side and reveals Cara, sitting on the piano bench with tears streaming down her face. She looks destroyed, sodden, as if her whole body is sobbing. Her shoulders are slumped. Her pretty face hangs like wet laundry.

"How did they know about our room?" Aimee hisses.

"Shh," Meghan whispers. "No idea."

They watch as J-Bar rants back and forth in front of the window, offering them brief glimpses of Cara, who never moves, never says anything or shifts position, just sits there facing forward and gushing tears as J-Bar's anger rains down on her from all sides.

It's a mirror moment.

Time splits as Meghan watches Cara implode under the impact of J-Bar's rage. It's seventh grade, the crowded hallway outside home-room, and Meghan is Cara, standing outside the circle of boys, looking past their huddle of haircuts into the center where Cara is Meghan. Meghan/Cara can't tear her eyes off Cara/Meghan. Cara/Meghan undulates in the shock waves of J-Bar's anger, sways away from him in slow-motion ricochet every time he leans into her face. She covers her eyes to protect herself against him, shakes all over. She is dangerously alone. He is dangerously angry. If no one comes to her rescue, she could be eaten alive.

For a long minute Meghan just sinks into the revenge. She can taste it in her mouth, brassy saccharine sweet. *Traitor,* she thinks quietly. *You brought this on yourself. You deserve to feel what I've felt every day since you abandoned me.*

Then a new numbness starts to spread through her. It's not the blurry numbness of invisibility, or the buzzing numbness of eating herself unconscious. This is a perfect hollowness, the zero feeling of watching someone get tortured—someone who is not you. Meghan feels the cool safety of standing outside. She feels the space between herself and the violence, dry as a breeze against her skin. She can sense every inch of the distance separating her from this scene—this scene that she dreamed up and set in motion and made real.

J-Bar heaves to one side to pound the wall with his fist, and something makes Cara look up through her fingers and meet Meghan's eye on the other side of the door. Cara's face flies open—a look of wild desperation—and her mouth opens slightly to say Meghan's name.

"She sees me," Meghan whispers to Aimee, her lips barely moving, her voice constricted. She's riveted to the ground, staring into the practice room as if entranced.

"So duck," Aimee whispers back, but Meghan doesn't move. "Hey!" Aimee tugs at Meghan's sleeve, trying to pull her out of sight. "Get down!"

"We have to go in there," Meghan murmurs, her pupils dilating.

"What are you, crazy? What are we gonna do?"

"She needs our help."

As Aimee watches, Meghan straightens her shoulders, shakes the hair out of her eyes, crosses the art hall, and yanks open the practice room door.

"—your idea of some sick freaking joke?" J-Bar's furious yell pours out as the door falls open. "What did I ever do to you, bitch?"

J-Bar perceives that something has changed behind him and spins around to face the door.

"Stop," Meghan tells him. Another Meghan voice Aimee hasn't heard before—hard and smooth as a slab of granite.

"Butter Ball, what the—get the hell out of here or I'll beat you to within an inch of your sick life."

"I said leave her alone," Meghan commands.

"Did you *hear* me?" J-Bar pulls his great height up to loom over

Meghan. Aimee stops breathing and flattens herself against the art-hall wall. She winces, bracing for what will come next. But Meghan looks up at J-Bar with pure fearlessness, as if she's never even heard of the idea of fear, never been afraid a moment of her life. Aimee watches, transfixed, as Meghan seems to expand, to widen and grow taller, as she refuses to back down.

"I'll scream," Meghan says, so so quietly.

J-Bar's mouth splits into a wolfish smile.

"Right," he scoffs. As if she had just said, "I'll fly."

Meghan opens her mouth.

In a fraction of a second, Aimee realizes that it's going to be the loudest scream she's ever heard. She claps her hands over her ears just in time for the piercing sound to soar out of Meghan's body, a sharp, singing blade of noise. J-Bar recoils as it razors through him. He wraps his long, tanned arms around his head, knocking his maroon baseball cap to the floor, and screws shut his eyes. J-Bar curls away from Meghan, who seems to be growing even larger as she screams, and presses himself against the cinder-block wall. The scream detonates around them like a sonic boom, surging through the air of the art hall, barreling into the lobby and through the door of the main office and out the front doors of school and into the parking lot, louder and louder and louder and louder . . .

The scream wipes through every cell of Aimee's body. It lasts for a day, and then a month, and then a year.

Finally: abrupt silence, ringing with reverb. Staring dead ahead at J-Bar where he's cowering against the wall, Meghan opens her mouth and breathes in to do it again, a great gathering inhale.

J-Bar looks, squinty-eyed, from openmouthed Meghan back to openmouthed Cara—and runs.

He takes the art hall in five leonine strides, pounds through the doors at the end of the hall, and escapes.

His maroon baseball cap lies where it fell, on the tile floor at Meghan's feet.

The noise Meghan made is still echoing around them—J-Bar's crackling energy is still rippling around them in the air—when Cara gets to her feet. She smears the tears off her cheeks with the backs of both hands and takes a shaky step toward Meghan.

"You saved me," Cara says. Her voice is thick with crying.

Meghan doesn't move. On her wobbly legs, wiping at her eyes, Cara looks like a lost child. She looks for a flash like the Cara Meghan remembers from her haziest long-ago moments of happiness. Cara reaches out tentatively to Meghan, a half-gesture, and says again, "You *saved* me."

Meghan manages to shake her head, ever so slightly.

"Yes you did," Cara insists. "He was so, he came and found me out of homeroom, he was so mad, he practically dragged me here, and then he was yelling terrible things at me, and I tried to tell him I didn't know what happened—I *don't* know what happened, I didn't write that, I don't know who put that on the announcements, did you hear it? It wasn't me, though, I would never—who would ever do something like that? Who would ever do a horrible thing like that to someone else?"

Meghan feels the edges of her body start to shimmer in an

unfamiliar way. It's not that she's becoming invisible—she can feel Cara looking at her, *right* at her, for the first time in years—but what Cara's seeing as she looks at Meghan isn't real. She's seeing a savior, and Meghan's a saboteur.

"Did you hear it?" Cara asks again, coming another step closer to where Meghan is lodged, motionless, in the practice room door. "Do you know what I'm talking about?"

At her left elbow, Meghan feels the air eddy. Cara shifts her gaze to the space beside Meghan, and her eyes narrow.

"What are *you* doing here?" Cara says tightly. Meghan turns to look at Aimee, who has come to stand beside her. Aimee folds her stick arms across her chest—all points and corners—and doesn't answer, just stares Cara down. Meghan looks back at Cara and watches the figuring-it-out play on Cara's face like a silent movie, a gradual morphing of her expression from grateful damsel-in-distress to wounded martyr to outraged avenger.

"You . . ." Cara's petal-pink mouth works to form words, comes up empty. "You . . ."

"You shouldn't have copied," Aimee says, emotionless.

"*You* did this? To punish me?" Only two feet away from Meghan, Cara begins to vibrate with rage. Meghan slides an inch to the side, and another inch, trying to extract herself from the center of what she fears is about to be a shattering confrontation.

"I didn't want to punish you, I just wanted my poem back. It wasn't yours and you knew it." Aimee's careful, controlled voice gives Meghan a slight chill. She drifts another couple of inches to the right, so she's half in and half out of the practice room doorway.

"Why didn't you just *talk* to me about it?" Cara is almost screaming. "Why didn't you just *tell* me you were mad?"

"I did tell you—in the parking lot after the *Photon* meeting I talked to you about it and you wouldn't listen. You said I didn't own hungry."

"Well you don't!"

"You copied," Aimee says flatly, shrugging her knobby shoulders as if that settles it.

"You humiliated me in front of the entire school! How am I supposed to go to class when everyone—and you—you don't even know J-Bar, why would you bring him into it? And how did you even know about that stuff, the shed and the—"

With an almost audible *ping* the last piece of the puzzle falls into place in Cara's mind; she flinches as if someone has flicked her on the forehead, and turns a startled look on Meghan, who has floated so far out of the doorframe by now that she can only see Cara with her left eye.

"You didn't," Cara says softly. Meghan feels her heart collapse in an implosion of guilt. She wants to offer a thousand apologies, to fall to her knees in front of Cara, but she can't move a muscle.

"I asked her to help me," Aimee interrupts. "It was my idea."

"How could you." Cara locks eyes with Meghan. "I would never have thought you could do a thing like that. That's not you."

Meghan stands frozen, unable to respond.

"I just think you should know," Cara gulps, welling up with a fresh wave of weeping, "that even though you stopped being friends with me a long time ago I still care about you. You'll always have a special place in my heart. And I would never do something horrible like that to you. Ever."

At this Meghan feels the throb of remorse that has been growing in her heart shut off abruptly. The feeling just dies. Cara has no memory of what she did to Meghan. She's rewritten their history with herself as the victim.

One perfect tear slips down each of Cara's pink cheeks. Her face is a soft-focus portrait of innocence betrayed.

Meghan runs the possible things she could say to Cara through her mind:

I never stopped being friends with you, you left me alone when I needed you most.

You chose J-Bar over me even after you saw how he treated me.

I don't have a special place in your heart. You haven't even looked at me in over three years.

Cara whimpers and hiccups, clears her face delicately of tears with the tips of her two first fingers. "Don't you have anything to say to me?" she demands.

It's too much—Meghan's exhausted, and the challenge is too huge. She can't make herself say the words.

"You have everything," Aimee says, inserting herself into the silence where Meghan's response would be. "You have friends and awards and everybody loves you. All I have is my poems."

Cara pivots to turn a withering look on Aimee.

"I guess now you have *her*," she snaps, jerking her head in Meghan's direction. "You two deserve each other."

•   •   •

They stand for a moment in the empty art hall after Cara leaves, looking at each other almost shyly.

Meghan thinks, *I wonder what she wants to do now.* Aimee thinks, *I wonder what she thinks we should do now.* Neither of them says what either of them is thinking.

The project is over. They don't need each other anymore. They never have to speak to each other again if they don't want to.

"You want to meet here after school?" Meghan says finally.

"Okay," says Aimee. "What are we gonna do?"

Meghan shrugs. "You'll think of something."

• 19 •

They meet at the bench outside the front doors, blue wind-breaker and red velvet hat. Every morning now.

They go inside together every morning, side by side, keeping a careful distance between them but walking almost in unison, like a brace of soldiers.

They weave through the crowd in the entrance hall. They separate and come together and separate again, drift off slowly in different directions.

They meet in the sophomore hall during passing period, in the sickroom when they need a break from classes, in the art hall during lunch, in the music practice room after school. When they meet they lean their heads toward each other a little, murmur things to each other only they can hear.

Look from one of them to the other.

Look how different they are. Look how one is huge and one is narrow, one billows out and one sucks in, one is like a sea creature and one is like a spear. Look how when they walk together they make no sense.

Look how the same they are. Look how they both drop their heads when they walk through a crowd. Look how they both grip the shoulder straps of their backpacks with one hand like that. Look how neither one of them looks like anyone else in school.

Look how the fat one is like the answer to the question the skinny one asks.

Look at how no one looks at them as they pass. No one follows them down the hall anymore, no one stops them at their lockers. No one corners them in the gym or the stairwell or the parking lot. No one notices them as they wait for the late bus or eat their lunch together on the floor in a corner.

Look at the new way they've invented to be invisible.

Look at how they look at each other. Hard to see from a distance, but it's there: a deep, searching look. A look that notices everything it falls on. The look each one of them gives the other seems to make the other one real.

See how every second they're together, every second they're apart, someone is looking out for them now.

See how they don't need you to look at them anymore.

Lift up. Lift up so you're floating up by the ceiling of the front hall as school lets out for the day. Take in the whole mass of kids rushing like a flash flood toward the doors. See—they're in there, the two of them, bobbing along. Two heads in a rush of heads: velvet hat and mousy hair. Follow them until they blur, blend in completely with everyone around them.

Now pull back farther: the pebbly school roof, the parking lot, the football fields and soccer fields and the track. The multicolored flow of kids out the front doors, dispersing into the yellow tubes of buses, the rectangular tiles of cars. Trees on all sides turning brown, orange, gold. The breeze getting crisper and chillier up here.

Look up, look out: the town, the university, the valley deepening and darkening in advance of winter. A last wash of color before the snows come.

Now forget what's below you.

Look around you now: the sky is perfect blue up here, cold and pure and bright.

Float up here for a second, where it's flawless.

Now take a deep breath, and disappear.

Acknowledgments

For her wisdom, patience, and vision, I'm grateful first of all to my extraordinary editor, Joy Peskin.

For their support and generosity, both emotional and material, I thank my family: Katie and Steve George, and Jenny George and Kate Carr.

For leisurely time and exquisite space to write in, I thank Madeleine and Tim Plaut.

For their camaraderie, commiseration, and constant encouragement, I'm particularly grateful to Pam Cobrin, Rob Handel, Philip Kain, Nicole Wallack, Anne Washburn, Abby Weintraub, and Aaron Zimmerman and New York Writers Coalition.

A thousand blessings upon Carley Moore and Matt Longabucco for the giddy fun, good food, and challenging collaborations they share with me.

And for friendship that has spanned the years since seventh grade, love and thanks to Lorelei Russ and Nikola Smith, there from the beginning.

Turn the page for a discussion guide to
Madeleine George's

Discussion Guide

• Who is Meghan Ball? Who is Aimee Zorn? Describe each of their appearances as well as their personalities and characters. What three words, other than the obvious ones regarding their sizes, would you use to describe each of them?

• Compare and contrast Meghan's and Aimee's home lives. How do their home lives affect who they are?

• Mr. Handsley states that adolescence is "ethically complicated" (p. 59). Do you agree? Explain. Mr. Handsley further relates his class's work with the play *Julius Caesar* to "the endless drama" that plays out in the school hallways (p. 61). What dramas are played out in this story? How are they similar to and different from the dramas played out in your school?

• As Aimee talks about her first day of school over the phone to Bill, she describes what she saw J-Bar and his friends doing to Meghan in the hallway. Aimee tells Bill that she "couldn't believe no one was making them stop" (p. 30). Why was no one making them stop? Who could have, and what could they have done? Who is to blame for the bullying Meghan suffers at school? Why?

- Why is Meghan so invisible to others? Why isn't she invisible to J-Bar and his friends?

- Meghan collects information or as she considers it, "Facts about People." Why? What does this do for her? What message do you think Madeleine George sends regarding "facts" about people? Explain.

- What do you think about Mr. Handsley's advice to Meghan to stand up to her tormentors (pp. 219–220)? Do you agree or disagree that Jonah is better off for speaking up for himself? What do you see as Meghan's options for handling this bullying? What advice would you give her?

- Aimee feels tricked by Cara's poem "Autumn Elegy" (pp. 101–103). Why? Did you feel tricked? Explain your reaction. What do you think about Cara's assertion that "It's poetry. . . . It's art, right? As in artificial? You're allowed to make things up" (p. 103). Is art—poetry or any other form—artificial? Explain.

- Aimee claims that "No one has your exact same experience. Every single person's story is different" (p. 107). Cara claims that "You think you've had some special unique experience that only you can describe but actually a million other people have had that same experience, and they might describe it just the way that you would. . . . If we were all totally unique and special we wouldn't ever understand each other when we talked or wrote" (p. 152). What do you think? Who do you agree with?

- Does anyone own an idea? Explain. Look back at Cara's explanation of the ownership of ideas in the Photon collective on pages 44–45. Explain how this does or does not relate to Cara's defense of her award-winning poem when she tells Aimee, ". . . nobody owns ideas. Ideas belong to everybody" (p. 152). Do you think Cara stole Aimee's poem? Defend your opinion.

• What happened between Mr. Handsley and J-Bar in the *Julius Caesar* performances? Do you agree with Dr. Dempsey's feeling that Mr. Handsley should be disciplined for his actions? Why or why not?

• Discuss Mr. Cox and Mr. Handsley's ongoing feud. Have you noticed a similar push and pull between athletics and academics in your own school? Is one really more important than the other?

• What power did Cara have over Meghan in seventh grade? How was Cara able to make Aimee feel happiness? Why do you think Cara betrayed each of them? Was Meghan and Aimee's revenge on Cara and J-Bar justified? Explain. What were other ways, if any, that Meghan and Aimee could have handled their pain?

• As Meghan suffers from the memories of her younger friendship with Cara, the narrator reveals that she learned "that all promises are fictions, all friendships are games with winners and losers. . . . every human being has a value assigned to them that they are helpless to change no matter what they do . . . people trade each other like baseball cards: three cheap friends for two valuable friends, a whole group of worthless friends for one popular friend" (pp. 143–144). What do you think about these ideas? Do you see people treating friendships this way?

- Does Aimee have an eating problem? Does Meghan? Discuss their relationships with food. Are they acting out their emotions through their bodies? What in this story leads you to these answers?

- Throughout the novel, Aimee experiences what she calls allergic reactions and symptoms, indicating the onset of reactions. How do you understand these reactions? What is she reacting to? Why can she safely eat bread at Meghan's house (p. 200)?

- Who do you like in this novel and why? If you could have a conversation with any character in this story, who would you talk with, and what would you say to him or her?

- Envision Meghan and Aimee in ten years: Who are they? What do they do? What do they look like? What makes you picture them in this way?

- What does this story say about friendship? Revenge? Appearance?

- Madeleine George uses a writing style that brings the reader into the novel in Chapter One as an active observer who then reverses this entrance at the end. Why do you think she chose to do this? What does this do for you as a reader?

- Why do you think the novel is entitled *Looks*? What does the title mean? What other titles would you suggest for this story?